Snow Fence Road

Phyllis Edgerly Ring

Black Lyon Publishing, LLC

SNOW FENCE ROAD
Copyright © 2013 by PHYLLIS EDGERLY RING

Our books may be ordered through your local bookstore or by visiting the publisher:

BlackLyonPublishing.com

Black Lyon Publishing, LLC
PO Box 567
Baker City, OR 97814

This is a work of fiction. All of the characters, names, events, organizations and conversations in this novel are either the products of the author's vivid imagination or are used in a fictitious way for the purposes of this story.

ISBN-10:   1-934912-54-9
ISBN-13:   978-1-934912-54-6
Library of Congress Control Number: 2013941443

Written, published and printed in
the United States of America.

Black Lyon
Contemporary
Inspirational
Romance

For Jon, who believes, and whose kindness endures with such grace.

Prologue

It took Evan Marston three tries to find a tie without moth holes. Most of the holes weren't large, and two of the ties had never been favorites anyway.

He chose to wear the third because its tiny hole was hidden after he knotted it in place and because this tie had belonged to his father, one of only two he'd owned. The other had been buried with him.

Evan liked the idea of wearing something of his father's today, the first time he'd worn a suit in years, and the first in a long while that he'd done anything as public as attend a funeral. It should be easy since no one besides Claire was likely to know him.

The funeral was a five-hour drive away in western Massachusetts. That she had asked for his help at all showed how troubled she felt. Claire never asked, and always found some way to put you off if you volunteered. He had been surprised when she'd approached him between the cluttered aisles of Dickie's general store a few days ago and said, "My mind's so flummoxed. I don't trust myself to drive."

He'd been so happy to say yes. Absolutely nothing about the way Claire treated him had changed since his accident, though she, more than anyone, had reason for it to. She had been his only visitor at the hospital, and later at rehab, and those hadn't been easy visits, he knew. He'd been so angry and remote, shattered in every possible way. Claire was the kindest person he had ever known, the closest he had come, he supposed, to what it must feel like to have a mother.

Evan stepped back from the mirror to survey the length of his appearance. Since the dark wool slacks and jacket had been stored in cedar, they looked as good as the last time he'd worn them. The face looking back from the mirror was a lot less hopeful than the twenty-eight-year-old one captured in photographs the last time he'd worn this suit—on that day he'd mistakenly expected to be the happiest of his life. Thankfully those were photos no one had rushed to show him.

What happens, he wondered, to moments that turn out to be important for the wrong reason, and become things you don't talk about? He wasn't the first man to be stood up on his wedding day—well, rehearsal party. Just the only one he'd ever known. How glad he was that his father had missed that, and most of what had happened since.

The slacks fit well, but the jacket was snug. The exertion demanded of Evan's upper body over the last four years had shaped his shoulders and arms into a much broader form than the rangy build he'd always had. He gazed at his reflection as though this well-dressed man were someone else.

Then he turned to move and his constant companion, the limp, reminded him exactly who he was. He spent so much time in his own company that his awareness of this uneven gait all but disappeared—until he caught people watching him. Then he remembered that he passed almost nowhere unnoticed now.

He was running early but decided to head into the village anyway. He'd told Claire he would pick her up at the Spinnaker at eleven. He knew she'd understand if he got there a little early and waited for her in the Inn's parking lot.

As he nudged the old Volvo wagon out of his long dirt drive onto the shore road to the village, sea and sky stretched out in a single gray expanse, the horizon line indistinct between them. The air was saturated with a salty tang and raw cold, though the start of spring was days away and all of the winter's heavy snow had finally melted.

Evan knew little about where he and Claire were going. The funeral was for someone he'd seen a few times around Knowle, though the man wasn't a local. The guy had actually stopped a couple of years back here on Snow Fence Road to help Evan when a table he'd been hauling started to slip from where he'd strapped it to the roof of his car.

That had been after the accident, after he'd finally gotten home again and his human contact had been minimal. He must have looked like a hermit with his straggly hair and mountain-man beard.

But this man, Andy Hollinger, had seemed earnest and helpful and Evan had been glad for the hand. Now this good Samaritan was dead. Some kind of cancer, Claire had said. Evan knew Andy had worked for her one summer at the Spinnaker but her allegiance in attending this funeral went further than that, if he understood right. It was the man's fiancée who had Claire so worried.

Evan remembered her vaguely as one of the Maine village's thousands of summer visitors, talkative and rail-thin. Her only family appeared to be her mother, a small brown-skinned woman with a kind smile. Evan knew this fiancée, Tess, and her mother were like family to Claire, that mother and daughter came to the Spinnaker most summers and this was where she and Andy had met. Unlike so many summer regulars, Tess hadn't crossed Evan's path in the years since his accident. Maybe that was because she'd spent time at the Spinnaker at the point in his life when he'd so avoided it.

As he nosed the car into the Inn's lot, Evan saw Claire coming out the side door from the kitchen, hurrying away from the sprawling old wooden structure at her brisk pace, auburn curls tossing in the March breeze. He'd once teased her that she had "two speeds—here and gone." Nearing her sixtieth birthday, she still moved like a sprinter.

He had just swung his stiff left leg out of the car as he called, "Hang on now, Claire. Let me give you a hand." But she was too quick for him.

"Oh, I'm fine." She was already pulling open the passenger-side door and sliding into the seat beside him. "You're going to enough trouble as it is."

She wedged and tucked her bags around her feet. She'd packed enough food for several meals, he knew. "So we won't have to stop. Except for the necessary."

Evan smiled to himself. His father had called it "the necessary" too.

He took a sandwich from her gratefully as he drove toward the interstate and relaxed into the familiar comfort of her company. When he'd finished eating, she handed him a paper napkin and said, "You are so good to do this with me, Evan."

"I'm happy you asked."

Her breathing sounded labored, fast. She appeared to relax a little when she turned toward him, as if thankful for the distraction. "You look awfully fine," she observed. "Dressin' up suits you."

Over the past few years, Claire was one of the few people from whom Evan could accept eye contact and know there was nothing linked to it but her real regard for him.

He shrugged, the trace of a lopsided smile on his face. "Haven't had much occasion to find out lately, I guess."

He noticed she'd grown quiet and saw that tears were streaming down her cheeks. He pulled the car over to the side of the road, slipped it out of gear, and set the handbrake. Reaching to place a hand on her shoulder, he said, "I'm so sorry, Claire."

"Oh, Evan," she gasped with a small cry. "Why do these things happen? Why do people have to suffer like she's suffering?" Her eyes, watery with tears, met his before she dissolved in sobs she kept trying to stifle. "I feel so thoughtless, putting this all on you. You've already gone through more than anyone should ever have to."

Evan watched her, his heart stirring inside him like some small animal beginning to waken. "You're not putting anything on me, Claire. When these things happen, we do the best we can. You're going to help her. And I'm here to help you."

•

Twelve hours later, he was lying in a house where clocks ticked everywhere and at least two chimed the hour. The funeral had started at six that evening and so had the snow. When they'd exited the funeral home, the driving had been abysmal. "Please stay the night," Tess's mother, Pearl, had urged. Evan knew Claire wanted to have some more time with the two women and was relieved not to drive in the storm. Now he was lying on the couch in the cozy living room of Pearl's old Cape in the Berkshire foothills.

He'd felt like a camera during the service as he sat beside Claire, and watching Tess had loosened something in him. She must have been well-medicated, he supposed, encased in a distant, lonely aura, as though she wasn't there at all.

Through the window now, he saw that the snow had stopped. When his leg stiffened, he shifted around in search of a more comfortable position.

He'd just managed to find one when he saw the shadow, then sensed the presence standing directly beside him. Tess was weaving back and forth, her features intermittently visible in the moonlight that had begun to gleam through the window. Her expression was dazed, yet more conscious than a sleepwalker's.

Evan worried she'd suddenly fall, or that his presence might startle or agitate her. Did she know he was there? Had she even seen him today?

"Are you ... all right?" he asked finally as he slid slowly into a sitting position.

"I can't sleep." Her voice, barely audible, was flat.

As though the words had tapped the last of her reserves, she slumped suddenly and Evan knew she was going to fall. As he moved to intercept her, the only way to avoid the edge of the coffee table was to close his arms around her and guide her down until she landed beside him. Her head lolled as she came to rest against him, sliding down onto his chest until he reached to cradle it gently and move it back onto his left shoulder.

Evan struggled to sit upright but it was impossible. He sat wondering what to do as the moonlight shed soft pools of light on her pale skin and dark hair. He had no idea which room was hers and she certainly wouldn't be able to tell him.

She shivered with little gusts of tears that trailed off as she slipped into sleep then startled out of it like a restless child. He decided the best thing was to remain still until she fell asleep then find a way to disengage and let her rest here.

Instinctively, he stroked her hair, which seemed to have a quieting effect. "It's all right," he murmured. "You'll get through this. Even if you can't believe it now.

"Just rest," he urged softly. "There's nothing you could have done differently. Let sleep take you away for a while."

As he said these things, he felt a sense of peace he dimly remembered but would never have anticipated. In the days after his accident, there had been no one to console him and, perhaps worse, no one to console. This, he realized, is part of how people get through loss, though each goes through the needle's eye of grief alone. It was that great loneliness that had made him want to die or, more exactly, struggle to find the will to live—made life itself seem like the worst of punishments. It was odd to suddenly feel so close to that again when he'd worked hard to distance himself from it.

She lay heavy against him now. In a little while, he'd probably be able to disentangle himself without disturbing her. But for now, there really wasn't any hurry. The unexpected peace of this contact seemed to hold him in place.

Here he was with the last thing in the world he'd have ever expected—a pleasantly warm, fragrantly scented, and distinctly female body wrapped in his arms. You just never knew what you were waking up to some days.

Chapter 1

The bead-sized berry was a perfect shade of violet and nearly twice as big as the others Tess had picked so far. She paused to study it before palming it into her mouth, then glanced over her shoulder to see just how far she had drifted from Claire.

The other woman wasn't in sight, but she would sure be delighted to see these. Claire stalked every fruit in its season like a hunter, determined not to miss a single one.

In June, the two of them had been surrounded by mounds of strawberries that left rose-colored stains on every surface in the Inn's kitchen. Next they'd braved the barbed fortress of the blackberries. Now, when the heat rivaled Panama, Claire said that the blueberries couldn't wait. The bushes were interspersed in clumps between the craggy rocks above the shore, where an occasional breeze off the water provided only a tease of relief.

Tess's thoughts wandered as she dropped handfuls of berries into the enameled pail beside her. The sun beat down on her veil of dark hair as she worked steadily, absorbed in her rhythmic harvest. When she first saw the shadow, it took several seconds to identify its shape as human. Glancing up, she was shocked to find a man standing just a few feet away.

Everything about him was tawny brown: his face and torn khaki shorts, the arms crossed over a smooth wide chest, even the strands of golden brown hair the breeze lifted playfully. His eyes, an aquamarine of startling clarity, were fixed on her so hard she couldn't look away.

She staggered back several steps, stumbling on a rock. "Oh!" She pressed a hand against the pounding of her heart. "I never even heard you."

"I know." The light in his eyes widened for an instant; his gaze didn't shift. "I'm sorry if I scared you."

Her thoughts raced. He must have come out of nowhere. Maybe he hadn't wanted her to hear him. She groped for what to say as he continued to watch her. Then she noticed the roof peak looming from the crest behind him.

"Oh, goodness—is this your property?"

He nodded.

She took more small steps backward. "I'm … sorry. I didn't realize. I'll be right out of your way."

"You're not in my way." The corners of his mouth raised slightly. "And don't forget your pail." He gestured to where it stood not far from his bare tanned feet, then peered down into it and noted, "It isn't even filled yet."

"I didn't realize I'd wandered so far." Half of Tess was ready to bolt, the other half magnetized with both uncertainty and interest in those penetrating eyes through which light moved and sparked.

"As you like. But you're welcome to keep going, if you wish." He bent to heft the pail up. "May I?" He indicated the contents.

"Oh, of course. They're yours, after all."

He scooped up a handful and savored them slowly. "They're absolutely perfect today. You caught them at just the right time."

So Claire had been right after all, heat or no heat.

"By the end of the week, they won't be this sweet." He continued to look at her as though he were waiting for her to say something. But she seemed—paralyzed, unsure what to say next. After the initial jolt of finding him there, her scrambled confusion of awkward embarrassment was giving way to curiosity, and an odd sense of the familiar.

But here she was, trespassing, and that was no way to behave with Knowle's locals, especially when so many tourists invaded their town each summer. She stepped forward and extended her hand, finally. "You're very kind to share this good crop. I'm Tess Johansen."

As his hand closed around hers firmly for a second or two, she noticed he was still holding her pail and reached to take it from him.

"Enjoy your berries, Tess," he said with quiet finality and stepped back, turning to scan the direction from which she'd come.

She felt a small disappointment as she started away slowly. He'd been looking at her so intently, and then, when she'd introduced herself, he seemed to end the encounter abruptly. Perhaps he was just another private sort, like so many in this Maine town.

As she struggled along between the rocks, Tess glanced back and called out, "Thank you," to which he nodded slowly, his gaze still following her. Growing extra-conscious of her movements, she finally turned to toss one last wave but his back was toward her as he ascended the incline. She caught a final glimpse of him before he disappeared over the top of the ridge.

The unexpected irregularity in his gait surprised her. With each step, he seemed to hold his left knee rigid, swinging the leg with deliberate stiffness. He'd exuded so much strength and presence as he stood there surveying her that this vulnerability seemed … wrong. She couldn't make the two images connect.

He'd looked at her so openly at first, as though inviting contact. If only she hadn't felt so tongue-tied and confused. Maybe she'd just been dazed from the heat.

He had seemed to tower over her, even once she was on her feet. The generously sculpted planes of his face rose above a strong jaw, and the corners of his mouth tended upward in a way that was pleasantly reassuring. And those eyes! What an aquatic contrast they were to the earthly color of the rest of him, and so expressive, as though everything inside him flashed through them.

"I was worried you'd found a bear in those bushes!" Claire's voice jolted her out of her reverie.

Tess laughed, glad to see the familiar face beneath the broad straw hat.

"Where've you been?" Claire gazed past her, curious.

"I'll tell you all about it in the car."

The minute Tess fastened the seat belt of Claire's small sedan, the other woman insisted, "Come on, now. You've got that flush that means you've got something to tell me."

"Have I?" Tess lifted her heavy hair off the dampness on her neck. "Must be the sun. I call this a day for lemonade in a hammock but some people would rather court sunstroke!"

"It's a crime to let berries this good go to waste. And don't try to get round the subject now! Where'd you get to, over there?"

"Oh, I started daydreaming and wound up in an enormous crop

of berries. Naturally I had to trespass to find them."

Claire's eyes were bright as she glanced away from the road to look at Tess. "What happened?"

"Well, I finally looked up to find a man standing there watching me. Then I got my wits back and realized I'd wandered onto his property. He was pleasant enough. Didn't say a whole lot, but there was something about him ..."

"He walked with a limp?"

Tess turned toward Claire, surprised. "That's right. Who is he?"

"Evan Marston." Claire drew each syllable of the name out slowly. "You've met him before. Do you remember?"

Tess shook her head. "Here in Knowle?"

Claire seemed to hesitate, then said, "Evan was the one who drove me down to Andy's funeral."

After a moment, Tess said. "Oh ... yes. That was kind of him. I don't really remember ..."

"I know, sweetheart," Claire said gently. "There's a lot about that day you probably don't remember, and that's a blessing."

The plummeting sensation stirred in Tess's chest now, the pressure building in her throat, behind her eyes.

Focus, focus on anything else but this storm that will suddenly come up so fast ... "What's he like, this ... Evan?" Tess forced the words out finally

Claire shook her head. "He mostly keeps to himself, now. Works as a carpenter, builds furniture. Shows up in town once a week, maybe. A few years back, he fell about fifty feet from a ledge above a beach just down the coast. My niece, Celia, was killed in that fall, but Evan survived it by some kind of miracle. There was a lot of nasty press about it, implying foul play."

"Foul play?" Tess's tone was incredulous. After six months of reading the *Knowle Village Weekly*, the biggest news she'd seen was of chimney fires and the road antics of intoxicated adolescents.

"Yes," Claire's tone showed impatience as she braked at a small intersection then turned onto the main road toward town. "Fools from city papers heard of it and then everyone was trying to make it all look like his fault. Only thing he did wrong was to love that girl too much for his own good."

Claire's voice seemed to catch in her throat for a moment. Then she declared, "As if he hadn't already gone through enough, they had to shred up what was left of his life. Fact is, nobody but Evan really knows what happened that day."

Something rallied in Tess's memory. She recalled her mother relating a story when she'd returned from a visit to Knowle several summers back. Something about an accident in which a young woman had been killed and the whole town had been stirred up about the man who was found injured beside her.

Her curiosity was so piqued she didn't know which question to ask Claire first. "How well do you know him?"

"Since the day his dad brought him home from the hospital, just about. My mother and older sisters helped him out, for a bit."

"His father?"

"That's right. His mother died having him." Claire ran a freckled hand through her dense curls. "Poor folks. He was always a nice kid. You know, the kind you like to have come around. He was like a part of the Spinnaker once. About the only time I see him now is when he comes into Dickie's store for supplies, and he doesn't have much to say."

"Nobody knows what happened?"

"Not to my knowledge, though lots of folks like to think they do. He's the kind who keeps things to himself and none of us who know him want to tread on his toes by asking."

They were approaching the outskirts of Knowle Village and Claire quickly changed the subject to dinner plans for the small inn the two of them ran there. "We won't get all that many folks tonight, since it's only Tuesday."

Tess voiced a potential menu: "There's lasagna, some haddock I can cook a few ways, a couple of steaks—that good mushroom barley soup you made. There's plenty of that left isn't there?"

"Sure. What've you got for appetizers?"

"Oh, a few things—those stuffed grape leaves, some shrimp, the soup."

"That's plenty. You cook and I'll help the girls with the tables."

"This is supposed to be your day off!"

"I know." Claire's grin was wry. "My mother would be downright appalled at the sweatshop you've made of this place."

As they unloaded the berries near the Inn's kitchen entrance, Tess mused, "I wonder how many ways we'll find to serve these."

•

Later that afternoon, she noticed there wasn't enough whipping cream for the blueberry pie she'd baked and hurried across the street to Dickie's store.

The township of Knowle, Maine, had three distinct sections, which Tess likened to a family. The Harbor, with its mix of large summer homes and boathouses was the member struggling to retain tradition. The Beach, which drew the largest numbers with its eclectic opportunities, was the upstart youngster. The Village felt something like a poor cousin. Village and Harbor lay in close proximity and seemed to band together against the ever-encroaching growth of the Beach and its crowds of people from "away." Residents of the Village and Harbor always breathed a little easier when winter's desolation set in and the Beach grew ghostly again.

Knowle Village's business district was composed of the Inn, post office, public library, a small branch of the Casco Bank and Dickie's store. Nearly as old as the Inn, Dickie's was packed in true general-store fashion, with an incongruous assortment of life's necessities because "you just never knew."

"Hiya!" Dickie's voice boomed from behind the front counter as the screen door slammed behind Tess.

Her eyes struggled to adjust from the brilliance outside to the dim light in the old store as she gripped the counter between them. Dickie's huge hands were carefully lining up a miniature menagerie of carved animals he was unpacking from a box on the counter.

Tess picked up a tiny harbor seal and turned it over, noting its smoothness and intricate detail. "Where did these come from?"

"Friend of mine carved 'em for my sister's shop near Brunswick. Made her a sign, too." He reached behind the counter and pulled up a piece of ash-colored wood engraved with the words *Fiddlehead Crafts*.

"I know he's got a slew of work already. I just asked him for these last week and he dropped 'em off this morning. He left some bigger pieces, too. Come see."

Tess followed his giant frame across the creaking wooden floorboards to the back of the store, noting with amusement the same rolling gait men in his family had no doubt possessed for generations. Dickie probably spent more time onshore than they had, but this rollicking fisherman's walk remained, along with the vocal twang you only found Down East.

He halted next to a massive beech rocker and, fetching a creased blue bandana from his back pocket, wiped his reddening face. Nearby was an oak cabinet, all pegged with wood, a row of small, precise drawers at the base.

Dickie nodded at her appreciative whistle. "Evan's got a touch like no one else. Tourists usually grab these things right up this time of year."

Her head snapped up. "Evan Marston?"

"Yup," he nodded vigorously. "Buddy o' mine. Known him since grade school. You met him?"

"I ... kind of ran into him. This afternoon." Tess ran her fingers along the arm of the rocker.

"Try it out."

She sat obediently. "Is this how he makes his living?"

"Well, he turns out this kinda stuff out whenever he's between jobs."

"What sort of jobs?"

"Finish carpentry. He's a wicked fine craftsman, and usually has a house job somewhere. Cabinets and such."

"He seems like a loner."

"Well ..." Dickie cleared his throat and looked at the floor. "That's just since his accident, mostly. He had some bad times."

Tess wanted to hear more, and Dickie loved to talk, but from where she sat, she could see people filing into the Inn already.

She leapt to her feet. "I came in here to do something about dessert and I'd better get moving."

"Sure enough. I've got some stock to unpack. You get whatever you need and write it down on the pad by the register."

That night, the Inn served more dinner guests than either Tess or Claire had anticipated. When the rush finally slowed near nine o'clock, Tess felt wilted by the heat as she helped clean up the kitchen.

She ducked out to the small garden in back, feeling a twinge of guilt that she hadn't been near it for days. The cucumbers resembled dirigibles as she gathered them up in an armful.

Her gaze swept along the back of the imposing pearl-gray structure as she turned around. Each time she looked up at an eave, or caught an unexpected view of the Spinnaker, her heart swelled with an enormous sense of gratitude.

The Inn had been in Claire's family for decades until, just two months after Andy's death in March, an estate settlement had threatened that. Tess had known exactly what she wanted to do with the money Andy had left her, the new life she wanted to find in that place where they'd met and fallen in love—the place where they'd been so happy together before he got sick. They'd even talked about taking over the Inn when Claire retired though, as Andy had joked, "I think 'retirement' might look something like dying with your boots on for Claire."

Something inside Tess glowed as she remembered Andy now. At times like this, he felt close, as though he'd just whispered those words to her again. And he was close, she knew.

It was those other times, the ones when the horrible details flooded back ...

She shook her head, yanking her thoughts into the present, to the evening calm out here behind the Spinnaker where the sunset's roses and corals spread out in the sky. Being here was better than any therapy; six long, absorbing workdays a week. And now Claire didn't have to try and figure out how to keep the place afloat.

A little later, Tess climbed the two flights of stairs to her apartment suite on the Inn's third floor. She filled the footed tub in her bathroom, peeled off her clothes, and settled in comfortably.

The crack in the ceiling overhead resembled a stick figure standing on tiptoe and she traced the outline of its shape on the side of the tub absently, savoring the moments of peace as she lay immersed in the rapidly cooling water.

The air was still sticky when she decided to turn in early and she tossed about restlessly. When sleep finally came, it was besieged by dreams unpleasant and eerie.

She was running with leaden legs down a narrow hospital corridor. Over and over, she heard the sound of dishes and silverware crashing to the floor and felt the strong sense that she would be able to get there, this time.

Finally, she reached the door and threw it open but the room was empty, the bed stripped of its linen. Too late.

As she turned to leave, a tall cliff hung over her threateningly where the door should have been. She was standing on a beach now that stretched endlessly to either side and all around, pails of blueberries lay smashed on the sand.

Chapter 2

The Spinnaker Inn began life in 1870 as 91 High Street, an imposing Second-Empire home with a mansard roof built to house the extensive family of Harris Randall, an official of the Boston and Maine Railroad. Toward the turn of the century, one of his sons saw fit to mold it into a small inn. This effort to capitalize on the overflow from the gaudy "painted ladies" of Knowle's nearby beach resort was only moderately successful.

When the gay nineties passed, the building became more of a boarding house. Originally called the Randall Hotel, it was dubbed the "Randy House" in deference to its questionable reputation, and to the ginger-haired barman who later ran it.

Many of the village's older residents had vivid childhood memories of the house's Saturday night activity in the late 1920s. Dancers had crowded the ballroom until dawn while bootleggers kept the customers happy from big, shiny cars that lined the driveway.

A series of owners followed in the next few decades. The rooms stored potatoes during the Depression, and housed the residents of a home for the aged during the period just after World War II.

The house had stood empty for years as the result of problems with an estate settlement when Claire's mother, Dorothy Farragut, had bought it in 1960. Her eldest son helped her work a deal on the property and all five of her children pitched in to help restore the place to something of its former dignity. It was her daughter, Claire, who named it the Spinnaker, and was her mother's greatest bulwark through the years.

As Tess peered out the oval window of her third-story bedroom, the steamy heat of August's berrying seemed a distant memory on this crisp September morning. Sunlight streamed in as wind tossed the trees dappled with the same rosy red as the apples heaped in baskets in the pantry. Claire had started the kitchen's wood stove and its fragrance was wafting up the stairs, along with the salty aroma of bacon.

Tess dressed slowly, braiding her dark hair in a long cord. Remembering the new chill, she reached for the heavy wool cardigan she wore three seasons of the year.

The kitchen was empty when she arrived downstairs. Claire and two helpers were still in the dining room clearing tables and only a few customers, local workmen, remained. They nodded as Tess peeked out through the swinging door then resumed mopping egg yolk with their toast.

She checked the blueberries she'd taken from the freezer the previous night and pulled down one of Claire's dozens of cookbooks from the old china cupboard near the stove. She stockpiled ingredients on the oak table in the middle of the kitchen and proceeded to mix a large bowl of batter.

After filling several muffin tins, she placed them in the oven and pushed back her sleeves to tackle the dirty dishes towering beside the sink.

"Don't you dare!" Claire's tone was unyielding as she burst into the kitchen and seized a dirty platter from Tess's hands.

"I'm only going to load the dishwasher."

"Not on your first free morning in weeks, you're not. I've got the girls to help, you mind your business."

"I'm trying to! Guess I've got to let you show me up instead."

"Good little crowd this morning," Claire said. "Leaf-peepers, mostly, trying to tell me how much I don't know about Vacationland."

She moved to the oven and peered inside. "Why, you perfect sweetheart! These are just what I've been dreaming of all morning." The plates clattered as Claire rinsed and stacked them. "All that rush and I hadn't eaten a thing. Surprised I didn't drool all over those folks."

Tess smiled fondly as she watched Claire bustle about the kitchen, the red curls of her fiery halo subdued under a fleece headband the color of a blue spruce. What would she do without the bossy efficiency of the Spinnaker's real manager, the one who knew its every nook and eccentricity, who had grown up in them? Throughout the steady stream of college students who were never as sure about staying through Labor Day in August as they had been in May, there was always Claire, with her steadfast dependability, her knack of producing instant extra hands from some vast underground pool in the Village.

"Summer's gone already," Tess sighed.

"Get used to it, kiddo. Winters here make you forget there ever was a summer."

"Well, Greenfield wasn't exactly the tropics, you know!" Tess moved toward the swinging door that led to the Inn's front entry. "Need anything? I'm going to check the mail."

"No, thanks. I've got an errand to run after I finish up here. I gave the girls some work in back. They'll hear the bell if anyone comes in. How much longer for the muffins?"

"They'll need about eight or ten more minutes—I've set the timer. Save some for me!"

"Only if you're quick!" Claire called after her.

As Tess stepped down from the porch, the sounds of an old white Volvo station wagon broke the morning stillness. Rumbling slowly toward Dickie's store, it pulled into a space in front. Tess watched idly as the driver pushed the door open then froze in place by the Inn's hedge when she saw his face.

Swinging his left leg out stiffly, Evan eased up onto the right, then tossed the door shut behind him and limped toward the back of the car. He wore a dark turtleneck sweater and his right knee poked from a hole in his corduroy pants.

Opening the hatch door at the back, he removed a ladder-backed chair as Dickie came out to join him, taking the chair as Evan reached for a large box. The bellow of Dickie's greeting was audible as they disappeared inside.

Charged with electricity, Tess raced to the post office, several hundred yards past Dickie's. She yanked out the contents of the Inn's mail box impatiently and tucked it under her arm and hurried back out, half expecting him to be gone.

But the car was still there. When she reached the bench in front of the store, she sat down suddenly, hitting it hard in her nervousness. As she tried to focus on the mail in her lap, she began mentally rehearsing what to say.

Claire's tall, angular frame appeared across the street. "Walk too much for you, was it?"

Tess giggled, grateful for the words, and the face that was so much more familiar than the one she was waiting to see. "Thought I'd catch the bus to Bangor, actually!"

"Your muffins looked ready so I set them out to cool. Stay out of trouble," Claire called over her shoulder as she strode off in the direction of the harbor.

Tess waited restlessly until her eager peripheral vision saw him at last. Dickie's screen door slammed loudly as Evan moved toward his car, a box of supplies under one arm and a can of paint hanging from the other.

Tess waited as he loaded them into the back. Then, feeling a little like a lamb to slaughter, she rose as he walked round to the driver's side.

"Hello ..." she called out tentatively.

Her heartbeat seemed to pound through the pavement as she watched his head snap up, his shoulders stiffen slightly. A palpable flush passed over her when his eyes found her. Some of the tight lines around them disappeared as he let them widen.

She ventured further. "It's me—the intruder who poached your berries?"

He probably didn't remember at all.

Recollection passed visibly over his features, softening them a little. "Yes, of course."

"This is quite a coincidence," Tess rambled on nervously. "I just made some muffins with the last of those berries this morning. How'd you like to sample the crop?"

When he reached to stroke his jaw, she noticed what his sweater had masked: an inch or so of new beard a shade darker than his hair.

"That's ... very kind of you."

Of course he'll refuse. Whatever was I thinking?

"I haven't had breakfast and can't think of anything I'd like better."

Tess froze in shock at this virtual torrent of words where she'd expected curt refusal. "Wonderful," she blurted out finally. She gestured toward the Spinnaker. "We could have them on the porch, unless you think it's too chilly ..."

"It doesn't get chilly till January." Small dimples formed on either side of his mouth. "The porch sounds very nice."

"Coffee be all right?" she asked as he fell into step beside her.

"Absolutely."

The keys in his pocket jangled as they crossed the street.

"Please make yourself comfortable. I'll be right out," Tess told him when they reached the porch, then dashed inside as rapidly as though she'd left him bleeding to death.

She grabbed things from all directions, assembling them on a tray, then poured the coffee into her favorite silver carafe and snatched the cloth from a small side table in the foyer. She hefted the tray with care, pausing to compose herself and take a last look in the hallway mirror.

Her thick braid was starting to frizz, as though she'd just come in out of the rain. And here she was in her old sweater. Well, it wasn't as if there was time to do anything about it.

He was seated at one of the porch tables rubbing his lame leg as he watched the street. When Tess pushed the screen door open with her hip, he turned to face her and began struggling to his feet. She urged him to sit as she set the tray on a chair and spread the cloth on the small wooden table.

"You're going to a lot of trouble. This is finger food, after all," he said with a small smile.

"It's my pleasure." Tess arranged things on the table, moving the plate of warm muffins closer to him. "Help yourself."

He spread the cloth napkin she'd given him on his knee and pushed back his sleeves, revealing smooth forearms still summer-brown. Then a muffin disappeared beneath his hand as he transferred it to his plate.

Tess watched as he halved it neatly and added butter.

Her mind scanned frantically for the vital ingredient she had surely overlooked as she realized that she hadn't even bothered to taste these first. Muffins were always such a shot in the dark. At least these had risen up nice and tall, she noticed, then lapsed into doubt once more. Probably used far too much baking soda. Just the thing to nourish a hungry stranger. Some nice antacid muffins.

"Dickie showed me some of your work," she stabbed out at light chat. "It's quite beautiful."

He smiled his thanks at her over his coffee. Cupping one hand under the other, he sampled the muffin. "And yours is delicious.

Best way I know of to use those berries."

Tess released the breath she'd been holding and thanked him. She sipped her coffee as she stole glances at him while he ate and that riveting gaze wasn't trained on her so continuously. A knot of muscle moved in his jaw as he chewed slowly. Small waves of tawny hair curled above his ears.

His shoulders squared as he settled back in the wicker chair and that gaze caught her off-guard again when he leveled it on her.

"You must be the new innkeeper?"

"That's right." She was trying to spread hard chunks of butter on her crumbling muffin without success.

"I should have realized I was missing something when I heard Dickie was by-passing his mother's cooking to have breakfast here."

"Is he really? And I've heard she's such a good cook, too."

He nodded as he finished his mouthful. "I used to fish for lobsters with his dad. The incentive for getting up at four in the morning was that Maudey would fill you so full of good food you could hardly walk."

"Maybe I should go there for breakfast."

His low soft laugh surprised her.

Her expression was curious as she stirred her coffee. "Funny. You don't quite look like a lobsterman."

"It was a long time ago, in high school." He settled his chin in his hand. "What do I look like?"

She pursed her mouth as she studied his sculpted features, then shrugged. "Oh, a writer maybe. Or some other sort of artist? A musician?"

He continued to watch her in silence, as though considering her words, then said, "Well, you come nowhere near most folks' stout image of the village innkeeper."

"Oh, I'm working on it, or at least the scale says I am." She offered him the muffin plate then helped herself to another. "I hear it's almost impossible to cook for a living without getting bigger."

"How did the summer go?"

"Shortest twelve weeks of my life. I had no idea what I was in for, and it was probably better that way. That's what I get for being impulsive." She plucked crumbs from her sleeve. "Still, if rational thinking had had time to prevail, I probably wouldn't be here at all."

"That would be the Spinnaker's loss—and Claire's."

Tess paused in mid-bite, surprised to hear him mention her friend. She flashed a quick smile of gratitude. "And mine, believe me. I'd like to think I'm more than just another transplant from Massachusetts. You know, the kind some locals have a not-so-nice name for."

"Not this local," he protested. We need our visitors—and our transplants." Then he asked, his tone curious, "Were you doing this kind of work there?"

Tess hesitated before she answered. "No, I was working in a hospital."

"Ah." He smiled. "Trying to overcome those limitations of institutional food with your good cooking—"

"No, as a nurse," she broke in quickly to correct him.

"A nurse?"

"Yes, a very tired one, I'm afraid. Getting crisp around the edges."

While her tone had remained conversational, her insides felt like they were balling into a knot. "I ... waited too long. To leave it. By the time I did, it had all been ... wrung out of me. I think I stayed for some of the wrong reasons."

A shaft of shivery cold invaded her spine.

When she looked up finally, Evan's intent expression encouraged her to go on.

"You know," she realized, "this is the first time I've said that out loud. Understood that's how I saw it."

"Truth stumbles out like that sometimes."

"I guess it does."

She felt no urgency to break the silence that followed as birdsong and the breeze in the leaves overhead, Knowle's small morning sounds, enveloped them. She settled back in her chair and gazed out at the street.

"You were a wonderful nurse."

The suddenness of these words, and the conviction in his resonant voice drew Tess up straight. Her mouth went dry as a heavy ache of tearless grief filled her throat.

How could he possibly know how much she'd doubted that? That she'd left it all, in the end, because she couldn't make herself believe that anymore, and was terrified that in her frustration and pain she had forgotten how to be a good person.

"I developed a pretty keen ability to spot them, you see." He tapped his brow bone. "It's in the eyes, or something. But it's there. Every time." He shook his head. "I don't write myself up as an authority on anything but I learned that much pretty quickly, through painful necessity."

Tess met his eyes. "Well, I hope you're right." Then she reached for the coffee pot as she noticed his empty cup. "Will you have some more?"

"No, thank you. That was perfect."

"I seem to be doing all the talking here," she told him. "But then, you're asking all the questions!"

He laughed. "I guess it's your turn, then."

"Have you always lived here?"

"No, but I've always come back here. I suppose it's a kind of home port for me." A shadow passed over the eyes he raised to her.

"Where else have you been?"

"Oh, I worked with a cabinetmaker in North Carolina—near Asheville—for about a year. Spent a couple years at school in Boston, and had a summer in Oregon after working my way across the country. I visited a friend who lives outside Heidelberg and used his place as a base while I wandered around Europe on my thumb. Got the chance to work with some amazing woodcarvers in Spain. That's about the closest I came to staying away, but there were ties, you know." He exhaled a forceful sigh and his voice deepened. "The kind that have a way of pulling you back."

A church bell broke the silence eleven times.

He folded his napkin and set it on the table. Using the arms of the chair, he pushed himself to his feet. "If that painting I planned is going to dry in time, I suppose I'd better go get it started."

He grimaced as his left leg accepted the weight he shifted onto it. "Must've sat just a bit too long," he told her with a tight smile. "Thank you for the hospitality, and for feeding me so generously."

"I'm glad you came, Evan."

He shook his head apologetically. "I never had the courtesy to introduce myself, did I?"

"Oh, others did it for you."

He smiled, then wondered, "What else did they have to tell you?"

Her gaze was steady as she told him, "I generally take very little of what's secondhand into consideration. Only what's positive, and there was quite a bit of that."

His smile softened his features. "You've made far better use of those berries than I've ever done."

"Thanks. I'll see you."

His eyes were bright. "I hope so."

There was a soft, uneven thump as he made his way down the wooden steps.

Tess watched him amble across to his car. Long after its low roar died away, her eyes still watched the street.

•

Rowan Kearsage's pre-Revolutionary saltbox was tall and narrow. The half-acre on which it sat bordered Knowle Harbor, once the town's most prestigious section.

He painted almost as many pictures of the harbor as he did portraits, which had always been his livelihood. You could lay his harborscapes side-by-side and compose a complete mural, so thorough had he been in capturing every angle.

In his 74 years, he had seen much of his world and been close to its history as he'd painted the faces of politicians, millionaires and celebrities. After his wife died, Stephen, their youngest child, established a gallery of his own. Rowan left New York to re-explore a little town on the Maine coast where he had once spent the happiest summer of his life. As Tess understood it, Rowan's rediscovery of Knowle had ended any desire he might have had to return to Manhattan.

She paused near the front gate to his yard, eyeing the last brave sloops that remained in the harbor. She would miss seeing them in the winter months ahead. The water was a deep navy today. The shrieking gulls nearly drowned out the putter of the lone lobster boat making its way out of the harbor.

This was her favorite place in the whole town and she came as often as the Inn's busy schedule allowed. She had met Rowan during one of these excursions, when he had set up his easel outside, and they had been friends ever since.

"It's me," she called as she let herself in his back door and wiped her boots on the mat. Gentle strains of Brahms filtered to her ears.

She joined him in his harbor-view studio. "You're all ready for me today."

Seated at his easel, he was applying fresh color to his palette. She urged him to sit as he struggled to rise for her kiss.

"I've decided this will be your Christmas present."

"Oh, Rowan, don't rush yourself." She shrugged out of her jacket and ran fingers through her dark hair, trying to tame its windblown wildness. "I love having an important excuse to come here."

"I've had people drumming their fingers over me all my life. I need a little pressure." He reached across the table beside him to retrieve some brushes.

In the general order of his rambling house, maintained largely by Claire, this table was the one concession to Rowan's working nature. Towering piles slid haphazardly sideways on the littered surface. Tubes of paint and other supplies were heaped together with unanswered correspondence, books, magazines, tea-stained cups, and tired fruit that showed none of the freshness of that on his canvasses.

Out of painful previous experience, Claire had advised Tess never to disrupt, however slightly, any odd collection of objects she might discover on the various surfaces in Rowan's studio. "Still lifes." The words had a discarded sound. "He'll notice even the change you and I would never see, and it will drive him crazy for days."

Tess took a look at her developing portrait as Rowan studied it with her, a fistful of tiny brushes clasped in his left hand.

"This is gratifying work for me, Tess. Isn't genetics grand? The way it can shape Polynesian bone structure, fashion eyes that just miss being almonds, in a face with such pale fairness. Like Gauguin and Monet collaborating! Your parents did the world a service, creating beauty like yours."

"Hawaiian," she reminded, feeling slightly self-conscious.

"Ah, that's right—your mother was from Maui." He rubbed his eyes. "And your father?"

"Upstate New York. Near the Catskills."

"Yes, a very interesting marriage. Shall we have some tea?"

Tess nodded. "I'll go start the water."

In the sunny kitchen, she filled the kettle and set it on the stove. She'd become fond of Rowan's favorite Earl Grey and reached for the cream-colored tin where he stored it. She drew in a whiff of its perfumed fragrance then plucked a tea ball from the dish drainer and filled it about half full. She placed this in the indigo-colored teapot he kept on a shelf over the sink.

When she returned to the studio, Rowan told her, "There's something I'd like you to get for me upstairs, if you don't mind. I believe it's in the bookcase in the front bedroom—a book by Rilke, *Letters to a Young Poet*. Have you read it?"

She shook her head as she turned toward the steep stairs. Rowan no longer climbed them. A lonely day of pain at the foot of them after his hip gave out several years before convinced him he could now live comfortably in the downstairs rooms.

Tess scanned the bookshelf built into the west wall of the front bedroom and found the slender volume. As she turned toward the door, a stab of shock accompanied her sudden glimpse of the portrait on the wall behind her.

She moved closer to study the aqua eyes. The face and hair were the same golden brown—there were the same strong neck and broad shoulders.

What was different? Evan's face was younger, of course. Possibly more … confident, looking back almost in challenge. Like a young lion, Tess decided.

She hurried back downstairs and barely had time to hand Rowan the book before the kettle shrieked. She bolted to the kitchen and snatched it from the stove so quickly that hot water splashed out the spout onto her hand. Wincing, she ran cold water over it at the sink before she reached for cups and saucers.

What was it about this man who seemed to be turning up everywhere lately? She was buzzing with nervous excitement.

Her hand still smarted as she carried the tray of tea things into the studio.

"Rowan—" She handed him his cup then seated herself before him. "When did you paint that portrait in the front bedroom?"

His brows drew together as he puzzled to remember. "Oh, the one of Evan Marston? That's one a young protégé of mine did of him when he was about twenty." He took a loud swallow of the hot tea. "Do you know Evan?"

"I met him just recently."

Rowan glanced from her face to the one on the canvas before him. His brush made a tinkling sound as he rinsed it in the glass container of paint thinner beside him. "He lived in that upstairs room for a while, after his father died."

"I thought his father had raised him."

"Oh, he did, but he died when Evan was sixteen. Evan found him one afternoon when he came home from school. Had a heart attack before he ever got to work, I guess. I'll never forget Evan's face that day." His own was pale as he remembered. "I've always thought that if he got through that, he's built to get through anything. I'm sorry to say that time has tested my theory, but he wasn't found wanting."

"How did he wind up with you, after his father died?"

"He was probably capable enough to manage on his own by that time but I encouraged him to come here. Pled my own neediness. I knew he shouldn't be alone."

"What about his family?"

"There wasn't much of that. An uncle in New Jersey, his mother's only surviving relative, died a year before Evan's father did. Every other member of his mother's family had died in a death camp in Poland during the war. I think that his father's family was outraged that he married a Jew and disowned him. None of them showed up for the funeral."

"You've known Evan a long time?" Tess asked.

"Since he was fourteen or so. Nearly twenty years, now." He scowled. "God! I am old!"

"You're ageless, Rowan." She smiled as she straightened her teacup in its saucer. "What do you know about his fall?"

"Move a little closer to the window, would you? The light's not all that strong today." His brush explored his palette. "How much do you already know?"

"Only that it happened, and that Claire's niece was killed."

There was a brief, barely perceptible change in his expression. "Then you have heard of Celia."

"Only that she died."

"They knew each other from childhood, she and Evan, and never seemed to be apart for very long." He shook his head slowly. "They spent a lot of time here with me when they were in their teens. This was a refuge, for her, I think. She was sadly overlooked in her own family, but she did have Evan. He adored her."

"He must miss her very much now."

Rowan's mouth was a thin, defeated line. "We all do." He applied fresh color to his brush. "Evan doesn't talk about any of that, I'm afraid."

"I gather there were ugly rumors?"

"Idiot papers practically had him guilty of murder, or manslaughter." His tone was angry as he daubed at the canvas. "I don't know a whole lot more about that day than you. Just the damage it left. That leg he drags around. A desperate mess in Celia's family, afterward. The way he isolates himself out at his place on Snow Fence Road."

They sipped their tea in silence for several moments. Tess looked up to find him studying her. "Now I've gone and made your face all sad," he said.

"I'm just thinking about how much you don't see when you look at someone."

He leaned forward and met her eyes. "That's just it, Tess. There's so much there people don't see. He's strong—got strengths it takes some people a lifetime to find. From the time he was very young, he's had a special understanding about people."

Rowan's eyes sparkled as he continued, "That's grown even deeper now. He needs friends who'll bother to understand just what he is." A wry smile crept over his face. "Someone who'll mend all those trousers with the right knee missing, perhaps?"

Tess glanced at him, surprised, and rolled her eyes. "Well, don't look at me—I hate to sew!"

"I think it's worth your pursuing, just the same." His eyes twinkled.

She left her chair to kneel beside him, squeezing his hand. "I'll bet it's getting very close to noon, isn't it?"

He glanced at the small clock beside him and nodded. "You need to go?"

"Yes. I'm sorry to be so stingy with my time."

"It's all right. Actually, I seem to be doing quite well using the photographs we took. Can you come tomorrow?"

"You bet." She kissed his forehead and moved to the door.

Chapter 3

A few days later, Tess hunched in the shelter of her poncho as she tripped along a village sidewalk plastered with burnished leaves. She reached her destination, the porch of an imposing Victorian house, just seconds before a fresh downpour began.

The hurricane that had been moving northward off the coast had unleashed its heralds. Rain, whipped by a rising wind, had been nearly constant for the last day, drenching everything. The house's new coat of apricot paint seemed even glossier now that the rain had soaked it. The porch floor and window sashes had recently been painted a deep mahogany several shades darker than the trim.

Tess hauled the poncho over her head and shook it out, then turned the front door's brass knob and slipped inside. She reached toward a switch and light flooded the foyer, then she opened the nearby closet door and draped her poncho over it carefully. The steady rhythm of a hammer overhead signaled that workers were here, as the realtor had predicted.

Nine months ago, the Tasker House showed none of its current splendor. Located on a village side street, this modest Queen Anne's paint had been peeling off in sheets then. The kitchen and bath had each been a hideous mess and the only occupants had been the multitude of bats on the third story. It was the classic haunted house that the Chamber of Commerce opened to the public every Halloween; the kind children hurried past on their way home from school.

When a dentist purchased the house with the intention of resurrecting it for his own use, Tess had hurried over to see the challenge that faced him. She had her own dreams for the

Spinnaker, though she knew it would take years to fulfill them. Her mother kept sending enthusiastic letters along with copies of a magazine about restoring old houses. Pearl had even proposed taking her next vacation in Knowle to help get things started but Tess couldn't quite face tearing things apart just yet.

It had been several months since she'd been inside the Tasker House and its transformation was even more dramatic than she'd anticipated. She roamed from room to room, kneeling to run her fingers across the pastel Italian tile in the hearth of the dining-room fireplace. The stained-glass windows showed deep jewel tones today, with the scant light from outside.

The overhead light was on in the kitchen and the whole room seemed to reflect it. Oak cabinet doors, some of which had originally half hung off their hinges, were now meticulously restored. The upper ones had glass fronts, and the stone sink had new brass fixtures, the countertop alongside it a huge slab of granite. The massive new stove was a home version of the commercial variety Tess longed to have in the Spinnaker's kitchen. On the counter beside it stood a stainless thermos.

Someone was whistling a distant snatch of tune and she heard the sound of footsteps descending the front stairs as she reached the front hall.

Tess's heart skipped when she turned to face him. Evan wore a putty-colored shirt and a pair of battered jeans with an inevitable hole in the right knee. She smiled to herself as she noticed this.

The noisy hammer was now a silent captive in the leather tool belt that circled his hips. He cocked his head, teeth very white next to the dark fullness of his beard. "Well! I didn't know I had company!" He gestured toward the foyer. "What do you think?"

"It's exactly what I ordered. I can move in by the end of the week."

The aqua eyes sparkled. "Maybe the good doctor is unattached."

"Oh, I couldn't possibly marry a man who inflicts that much pain for money."

Laughter welled in his throat.

"My folks spent years working on old houses like this," Tess told him as she glanced around. "Always dreaming that the result would justify not being able to find the phone or bathing by candlelight for weeks after Dad discovered that the wiring was going to take a little longer than a weekend to finish."

Evan's eyes showed both humor and interest. "Did you help too?"

"What choice did I have? Scrapers and paint brushes got to be more inviting than toys you had to keep packed up so they wouldn't get full of plaster dust!"

He laughed again. "It was fun though, wasn't it?"

"Oh, sure. It was a real kick trying to explain to my friends why we had a lumber yard where the living room used to be."

She saw the amusement in his eyes. "Something like this makes me believe it might all be worth it, though. The floor looks absolutely beautiful.

"Thank you."

"This is your work?"

"The woodwork restoration, yes, including the floors." He pocketed his hands.

"It must have been a huge job."

He shrugged. "Not so much work as time. This particular floor was in the worst shape since it got lots of traffic. It needed quite a few replacement boards."

"It all looks so new!"

He eased himself onto his right knee, surveying his work. "That's the trick you see, blending it all together so that it looks the way it did a hundred years ago. That's what takes the time."

Tess reacquainted herself with his handsome features. The contours of his cheekbones made her fingers want to explore them.

"I have some coffee in the kitchen. Will you have some?"

She nodded. "Sounds great."

He rose slowly and reached for his toolbox. She followed him to the kitchen. "Have you seen the upstairs?" he asked as he poured steaming coffee into the cup that had capped the thermos.

Tess shook her head and thanked him as he handed her the cup. "That's wonderful," she said after she took a sip. "I feel cold right into my bones today."

Then concern crossed her face. "Did you give away your only cup?"

"No, I keep another here." He reached for a green stoneware mug and filled it. When he turned back, his eyes captured hers and held them.

"Do you always look at people so directly?" The words tumbled out before she had a chance to intercept them.

He frowned, looking puzzled. "I—I don't know. I don't mean to stare ..."

"Oh, it's not that," she hurried to assure him. "It's ... well, I guess it's just not something I encounter a whole lot."

His gaze dropped away from hers.

"Oh, Evan—please excuse me," she pleaded. "Maybe it's time for you to ask me why I can be so blunt and tactless sometimes."

He glanced up with a smile.

"I didn't mean to make you self-conscious. I'm sorry ..."

"No—it's a fair question. Maybe it's because people can say a lot without words, and I'm spending so little time around them lately, I don't want to miss anything." His brows drew together. "I hope it doesn't seem rude."

"Not at all. If anything, it makes you seem like a wonderful listener." She turned to look out through the glass of the back door. "Have you much work left here?"

"Just some molding to put up. I should finish up tomorrow."

His voice sounded closer and she turned to find him right behind her.

"Will you have some more?" He raised the thermos.

She nodded and extended her cup toward him. "I've been thinking about using the ballroom at the Spinnaker for dances again," she said as he filled it.

"Really?" His expression grew animated. "There used to be great contra dances there. I played with the band sometimes."

"What did you play?" she asked.

"Hammer dulcimer."

The sound of the words fell on Tess's ears like the sound of the instrument itself, in clear, soft plunks. Tinny notes of a tune echoed in her thoughts: *I Never Will Marry*. It was a song whose words had always made her sad, though she had never grown tired of hearing them.

In her mind's eye, she could see Andy's smooth hands with their tapered fingers that had danced slender mallets across strings with quick precision. Gentle hands, ones that had later clenched so desperately around cold metal that they had to be pried—

The tight sting in her chest splintered as she finally drew breath and tore away from the grip of these images and memories.

"I've built four or five, but it's been a while. They do take time." The sound of Evan's voice was muffled by the roaring in her ears.

Then came silence and the sensation of something settling gently on her arm.

She blinked up to meet his clear, sea-colored eyes. It was as though they reached all the way inside, helping her find her way back into the room. She wanted to gasp with relief as they pulled her into the bright warmth of the kitchen with him.

Then his fingers flew off her sleeve instantly, as though he had trespassed.

Her jaw felt unbearably heavy, weighted with emotion, as though it was going to pull her through the floor.

"Yes ... I'm sorry." Tess reached for where she'd set her cup on the counter and took a long swallow, then began pacing as she struggled to keep herself in the room, connect with what he'd been saying when something had pulled her away like an undertow. "You build the dulcimers? I'd love to see them. I haven't ... heard one. Not for a long time."

Evan's eyes followed her as she darted about quickly, rinsing her cup in the sink and then recapping the thermos with it.

"The reason I brought up the ballroom." She grabbed at the topic to focus herself. "It's the floor." Her words were coming out in labored gasps. "I think it'll need some work before we can use the room. Would you have time to take a look at it?"

The deafening roar in her head was fading. Just looking at him made her feel safe, grounded. She was so glad that he hadn't asked—that she hadn't had to fabricate some sort of explanation.

His lips pressed together as though he were fishing for words. "Of course. I'd be happy to."

Rain drummed overhead as another deluge pounded on the roof and she turned away from him quickly. "When will this rain stop?"

He shrugged as he rinsed his own cup at the sink, then offered, "Would you like to take a look upstairs?"

"I'd love to." Perhaps it was the coffee, as much as the conversation, but she was still suffused with a restless energy that was making her quiver.

Evan moved toward a door at the far side of the room and

opened it to reveal the back stairs. "You go first. I take longer."

Tess hurried up the narrow treads and turned to watch as he climbed laboriously behind her and suddenly felt thoughtless. "Maybe you'd rather wait for me downstairs?"

His eyes flashed up. "Why?"

"Your leg."

"It's fine," he said. "Just been on my knees all day and it slows me down."

He joined her on the landing and as he reached behind her to flick on the hall light, his clothes emitted a faint metallic smell.

As he led the way and they wandered through the rooms, Tess made appreciative sounds at the appearance of the floors, walls and woodwork.

"I wonder why he's not going to have his practice here?"

"I hear he's pretty established where he is," Evan told her as he paused outside a large bathroom. Its fixtures were the brilliant blue of lapis lazuli.

"Oh, my!" Tess winced. "What a color!"

"Same as his Porsche." Evan's mouth quirked in a smile.

He limped slowly past the double vanity through a door to the adjoining room. A sigh escaped him as he lowered himself onto the newly upholstered window seat in the tower alcove of the master bedroom. Then he shifted sideways to make room for her.

She perched on the edge and watched his face as he rubbed his leg.

"Are you sorry to be finished?"

"What, with the work here?" He shook his head. "I'd rather be building furniture. But the bills keep coming, those reminders of how lucky I am to be walking." His expression was grim.

Instinctively, Tess dropped to her knees and laid a hand against his leg.

He stiffened a little as he watched her, then eased back.

She massaged slowly until she felt the tight muscles start to lengthen beneath her hand. Some of the tautness left his face and the aqua eyes regarded her lazily when she looked up to meet them.

"I have this reflex when I see people hurt." She dropped her hands and leaned back. "Silly attitude some nurses have, you know. That we can somehow make things better."

He smiled. "That's just what you've done."

"I suppose it's worse in weather like this?"

"Sometimes it's hard to tell what worse is," he shrugged. "It throbs like it's fit to explode when a storm's on the way. Then when the clouds finally do let loose, it feels like I've got about ten extra pounds strapped there."

"Have you tried oil of wintergreen?"

His brows raised as he shook his head.

"It's helpful, especially in damp weather." She grinned as she stood again. "Makes you smell like toothpaste, but it works."

"I'll have to try it." He inched forward slowly.

Tess extended her hand and his eyes showed surprise before he grasped it carefully and rose to his feet, giving her hand a small squeeze before he released it.

Wind was driving sheets of rain against the windows.

"Can I give you a ride home?" he asked.

"I was planning to stop at the library," she said as she started toward the front stairs. "I'd be glad for a ride there."

She retrieved her poncho from the downstairs hall and slipped it over her head as Evan made his way more nimbly down the stairs. He locked the front door then snapped lights off behind them on their way to the back of the house.

"I'll get this door," she told him as he gathered up his things and donned a bright yellow slicker.

After she had pulled it closed behind them, she splashed through puddles to the car he'd backed close to the house. He loaded his things into the back then ducked in beside her. The car came to life with a rumble after several starts and coasted down the driveway. The rear seat was down and the boards stored in back scented the air.

Evan stared past the slap of the windshield wipers, then gestured to a book on the dashboard. "Would you mind taking that in with you?"

"Sure." She glanced at the cover as she reached for it. "Gracious! Tolstoy?"

He nodded as he turned the car onto the main street. "I probably won't live long enough to read everything I'd like to."

"Well, you're getting the heavyweights out of the way, that's for sure." She tucked the book under her poncho and fumbled for the door handle as he parked the car at the curb outside the library.

"Thanks a lot. It's been nice to visit with you," she said.

"Likewise." He reached to lift the hood of the poncho gently over her hair, his fingers brushing her cheek as he did. "Stay dry."

Tess looked at the rain doubtfully before she leapt out. "I'll try."

As she sprinted toward the building, she knew that the racing in her heart had absolutely nothing to do with her exertion.

•

The librarian shot Tess a smile of recognition when she set Evan's book on the counter. The high-ceilinged rooms were warm as she laid her poncho on a steaming radiator.

The local weekly paper hung from a cane with other newspapers on a tall rack in the corner. There had been little opportunity for reading during the inn's busy summer and Tess had taken to stealing away here where she could relax without interruption.

She fetched the paper and moved a chair near the radiator so she could slip out of her shoes and press her damp socks against it. She felt a shivery flash down her spine when she recalled Evan's parting gesture.

How glad she was that she'd followed that impulse to go to the Tasker House. She imagined her mother nodding in approval. Pearl Johansen had imparted to her only child the conviction that while such promptings might seem mysterious, they were usually just what you needed to follow. "How else do we imagine they talk to us, the ones who try to help from heaven?"

As Tess turned her attention to the newspaper in her lap, the only sounds in the room were the radiator's efforts to keep it warm and the clock, which marked the quarter hours with quiet chimes.

It was when she rose to tuck the paper back in the rack that the thought insinuated itself, seemed to propel her toward the desk. "I'll just see if I can find them," she reasoned. "I don't actually have to read them."

She tried to visualize that summer morning at breakfast when her mother had shared the story of the unfortunate Knowle resident Tess now wanted to know so much better. *It was around the time you met Andy*, an inner voice reminded, the one always eager to recall anything connected with him—the painful one nothing seemed to silence.

So ... about four years before. After the librarian had given her the day's password for the computer, Tess realized she was now burning to read.

She had brought no computer with her to Knowle because she'd wanted a total reprieve from so many things. "I'll tell people you won't have time for email—or calls," Pearl had agreed. Tess had hoped to leave the pain behind along with technology and the contact it brought.

She took a deep breath now as she searched for the web site of the local *Village Weekly*. She typed in Evan's name then flinched at the headline that came up. *Two Plunge from Morrison Ledge.* The story related the known facts, some information about those involved, and indicated an investigation was pending. A photograph of Celia accompanied the articles.

Tess peered closely at the small, heart-shaped face with delicate features framed by masses of pale hair. Something about the eyes stirred a faint sense of familiarity. They looked kind, Tess decided, but not happy, even though she was smiling.

The following week's front page spelled out the discovery that Celia had been pregnant at the time of the accident. Ambiguous and somewhat accusatory quotes about Evan from her family were included, and an investigation was underway. It was noted that the severity of Evan's injuries precluded any statement on his part.

Further stories over successive weeks revealed that Celia had fallen first and that Evan's only statement was that they had fallen accidentally.

Tess sucked her breath in quickly when she clicked on a link to related stories that brought her to a Boston newspaper. The photograph, which must have been taken from above the beach, was starkly graphic. What was obviously a body covered by some sort of cloth was sprawled on the rocks. Nearby on the sand another form lay contorted and partly covered.

Tess shivered involuntarily as her throat grew tight and something told her that she had as much background as she needed. But she couldn't seem to break free of her horrified fascination now. She moved on to succeeding stories that, in the following days and weeks again made reference to Celia's pregnancy, noted that she had fallen first, and that there was evidence she'd been moving rapidly when she fell. As though fleeing some ... thing, perhaps. Some—

Tess shook her head to clear this unpleasant thought and continued reading. Again, the only comment attributed to Evan echoed what she had read before.

She felt a knot in her stomach as she closed down the computer. Everything was so inconclusive. Had he read these? She tried to imagine his thoughts and wondered what was missing. Was the child his? Several of the stories had indicated he had just returned from Europe—perhaps the trip he'd mentioned—prior to which he and Celia had shared a residence in North Carolina.

What had they been doing so near the ledge? Had it been an accident?

Wracked with regret at her choice, Tess dressed slowly for the walk home. Darkness was closing in outside. The trees cast formidable shadows as she dragged her feet beneath the haloed streetlights. Her heartbeat quickened several times when she caught the shadows' movement from the corner of her eye.

She struggled to recall Evan's thoughtful words, and the happiness she'd felt earlier.

These were continually displaced, however, by the image of Celia's sad, smiling fairness and the grisly photo with the bitter quote from Celia's father: "We're not sure what he was doing out there with her."

•

Wind howled outside as Evan sat up and switched on the bedside lamp. Tired of tossing uselessly, he stretched and rubbed his vision back to clarity, then checked his watch. Once again, it looked like four hours of sleep was his quota.

Nights of scant sleep were something to which he was well accustomed. If discomfort in his leg didn't rouse him, then it was something unpleasant from dreams he couldn't always remember.

Tess's friendly animation had stayed with him all through that day after they'd visited on the Spinnaker's porch. He had fallen into bed early that night and woken to brilliant sunlight at seven the following morning—the first full night he had slept since the accident.

He had been seized with semi-conscious fear, at first. The world must surely have ended for so many hours to slip past him. He had finally laid back, grateful in the knowledge that miserly snatches of sleep weren't a permanent condition after all.

Without a doubt, he had been hoping for a repeat of this same phenomenon when he'd retired this past midnight. But his mind was much too wakeful, too filled with remembering their time at the Tasker House.

He rose stiffly and moved to the bathroom and splashed water on his face, rubbing his beard briskly. He slid his feet into a pair of moccasins and reached for a heavy sweater. Moving to the woodstove, he stirred its dying fire to life, added another log, then opened the door to his workroom to get it warmed up.

He withdrew a small bundle from the drawer of his workbench and set it on top. Peeling back the piece of chamois in which it was wrapped, he revealed a miniature replica of the Spinnaker about five inches high, carved from cedar.

He ran his fingers over it, noting with satisfaction the detail of its features and the wood's pleasing smoothness. With a quick twist, he separated what were, in fact, two halves of a small box. Just a little more work on the roof and it would be complete.

Seating himself on the stool at his workbench, he reached into the drawer for a well-worn photograph of the Inn and smoothed it out in front of him to study its detail. Then he selected several small tools and began the painstaking etching that would produce tiny roof shingles.

This was a particularly intricate carving and his perseverance surprised him, as though he couldn't wait to finish it. When sleep had vanished long before dawn during these past few weeks, he had begun this little piece of work as an alternative to the reading he usually did.

Somehow, though, thoughts of Tess had now become an inextricable part of the carving, something he looked forward to as he worked.

He had felt confused, even disturbed, when he'd first reckoned with what seemed to be happening to him. He had closed certain doors so firmly since Celia's death that the feelings and thoughts about Tess seemed incongruous, maybe even a little disloyal. Their sensation, however, was too insistent to ignore, like blood returning to a frozen limb.

There was absolutely no semblance here of his infatuation with Celia. Tess presented too many things he hadn't been fortunate enough to encounter before.

With Celia it had been such dogged persistence—exhausting, really, at the end. All his energy had been focused on trying to make things better, trying to make her feel loved and cared for enough, even as she became more and more removed, convinced of ideas that increasingly had no basis in fact. He'd been in denial, struggling to preserve something that had been dying for too long. Part of him had known that it was useless, but the part that had loved her since childhood let her develop a dangerous dependence on him, even when he knew it was wrong.

The scars must have been well on their way to healing that day he'd stumbled on Tess in the blueberries. Something had given the day extra brilliance, had made him curiously perceptive, where he would usually have been preoccupied and perhaps missed her altogether.

When he'd seen the slight figure with the veil of dark hair, so oblivious of her surroundings, he realized what had been wrong with the day so far. He had wakened with all of his senses heightened, somehow, and been lonely, really longing for company for the first time in a long while.

It was the portrait at Rowan's that had made him feel that way, he realized now, had made him pause to take in the sight of her as one would an expansively beautiful rainbow after a sudden shower. He'd recognized her right away when he'd seen the canvas, then been stunned to find her on his land just days later.

When she'd raised her sunburned face to see him standing there by the shore, he'd been twice as surprised as she had. It was the same face he'd discovered in Rowan's studio—the one he'd studied in the moonlight that night after he'd driven Claire to Andy Hollinger's funeral.

He had, admittedly, been disappointed that she didn't recognize him, probably didn't even remember that night at her mother's house. There was probably a whole lot about that day's events she didn't remember, or was trying not to.

Her forthright friendliness both surprised and delighted him the day she'd approached him in town. He'd enjoyed every moment of watching her as they'd sat together on the Inn's porch, feeling quickened by her exuberance.

Something had communicated itself to him that day, had somehow assured him that here was safety, and freedom from the tangled hangover of the accident, which followed him almost everywhere. Her near-Asian eyes, the same blue as the last few pieces of his mother's Wedgwood china, had shone with a kindness that convinced him that her interest was unconditional, and real.

It puzzled him that while she made him feel so safe, he repeatedly sensed something else in her that lurked just beneath the surface. He'd felt it that day on the Spinnaker's porch, and today at the Tasker House he had known when he touched her that it wasn't his imagination. Something had coursed through her like a current, even as she had fought to control it. Her face had given her away much more this time, something in the eyes that lonely pain had pulled far away.

He'd felt as though he were looking in a mirror, then. It gave him a quick, telling glimpse of what he had felt in the last few years. It was curious to see it in someone else's eyes. It allowed him to observe it from a distance without hurting. He'd had a sudden awareness of the passage of time and how much it had changed him.

Some kind of barrier had begun to crumble inside him. He found himself wanting to tell her everything would be all right. Never before had he believed so strongly that this was true, though he knew just as certainly that she wouldn't hear him. Not yet.

By the time he finished his carving, lavender had infiltrated the midnight blue of the sky with the first rays of daylight. Evan closed off his workroom and put the kettle on. Inspecting his work one last time, he rewrapped it carefully and placed it in a small cardboard box. Then he moved to where his heavy woolen jacket hung and tucked the package in its pocket.

He would keep it in the car. One day, when he went into town, the time would be right. For this, and perhaps for much more.

Through the long years of solitude he had grown versed in patience. He'd discovered all too painfully the price of wanting too much, of forcing a thing before its time. Trying to have the meal before it's cooked was how his father had described the eager boy who, even in manhood, hadn't been very good at waiting.

Well he certainly had learned better than that now. In fact, he had gotten quite good at it, and that's what he'd have to do. Just wait and see.

Chapter 4

Shortly after Andy Hollinger's death, Claire's mother had died unexpectedly. When she'd called to notify Pearl and Tess, her news had made her doubly heartbroken.

The Spinnaker would have to be sold so profits could be split among five heirs. Dorothy Farragut had meant to update her will after it became apparent Claire was the Inn's real proprietor but never got around to it. Claire's siblings were determined to reap all they could by offloading the Inn, even if it was Claire's whole life.

Tess and her mother had come to Knowle, and the Spinnaker, since Tess's junior year in college. When they received Claire's plea for advice, Tess responded in ways beyond anything Claire could have imagined.

It was as though Andy himself suggested it, she told Claire, one of those times when she felt him comfortingly close even though life was such a desert of pain. The couple had been planning to have their wedding at the Spinnaker before he'd gotten sick.

Tess phoned to say she knew exactly how she wanted to use the money he'd left her—how she knew he'd want it used. In a venture that met two sets of needs, Claire's life at the Spinnaker was secured and Tess had a fresh start in the place she and Andy loved most, away from where she'd last seen his anguished face. That, Claire knew, was something Tess kept trying to step over like a crack in the sidewalk.

Winter in Knowle had probably widened that crack, because winter was when Andy had died. Back in the summer, the challenge of taking over the Inn on the threshold of its busiest season had helped distance Tess from what shattered her life with savage suddenness just months before. But when Knowle's first snowfall blanketed everything in six inches of glistening white, Claire recognized the new innkeeper's cabin fever, especially with only occasional guests and so little to do.

She kept her concern to herself until Rowan called her on it one day after she'd fixed his lunch. He was engrossed in a small still life and didn't look up as he asked, "How do you think our girl's doing these days?"

For confused seconds, Claire was plunged in a tangle of long-forgotten memories before she realized what he meant. She dropped into an overstuffed chair and studied the toes of her shoes, collecting her thoughts.

"Just as I thought," he nodded.

Claire scowled. "Old man, why do you ask me, if you're so confounded sure!"

"I respect your views, particularly when they coincide with mine, as you know. Old man indeed!" Then he added more gently, "I see how worried you are. She has lots of time for sittings these days, yet all she talks of is how much she wants to get done in that old place. She's as restless as a cat at the door trying to get out."

Claire shook her head. "She won't let me get extra help. Insists on doing the work of two people in half the time, instead. It doesn't matter how much she does, there's never as much as she seems to need."

He rinsed his brush and wiped it on the rag in his lap. "Needs company, I'd say."

"Oh, would you now?"

He bestowed the smile that could soften her heart, even when he angered her. His gnarled hand caught hers in a firm grip. "I ought to know."

In moments like this, the almost brutal handsomeness he'd possessed when he first came to Knowle thirty years before broke through the ravages that age and loss had etched his face. Claire had been twenty-five when she had first seen him and had never loved anyone else in quite the same way.

"What are you up to?" She eyed him warily. She already knew the answer.

His smile was secretive. "Lord knows, I can't play God after all, though I've tried." His face grew sober. "How I've tried."

His gaze wandered to the portrait of Tess on an easel beside him. "He finds all sorts of things to do for me here, these days. All sorts of work in the studio, especially." He smiled at her knowingly. "Did you finish getting those canvasses down?"

Claire nodded and watched him uncertainly. "The attic's a mess, but they didn't look too bad. They're in the front bedroom."

"How many?"

"About twenty, I think."

His navy blue eyes were brilliant as he squinted at the canvas before him and dabbed his small brush with fresh color. "Not nearly enough, but it will have to do." His eyes narrowed. "Damned fools probably have twice that many stuffed away some place."

"Then you should count yourself doubly fortunate for what you have."

"What we have," he said emphatically.

"Let's just say I have everything I need," she told him quietly. "Whatever I lost, I probably misused. Or it was never mine to begin with."

He looked away.

"Rowan." Claire's tone was firm as she waited for him to look at her.

His expression was guarded when he did.

"You remember, now. Your promise. You gave me your word. Nothing without talking with me first."

He settled back in his chair, his brush poised in mid-air as he watched her. "I haven't forgotten."

"Please see that you don't." She gathered her coat around her and rose to her feet. "Your lunch is getting cold."

•

The Inn's kitchen was toasty when she entered it a short while later.

"Everything all right in the art world today?" Tess cradled a cup of coffee where she sat at the kitchen table.

"That's no kind of lunch." Claire clucked her tongue as she shrugged off her coat. "Old Woman Rembrandt's just fine. Minding everyone else's business, as usual."

Tess smiled as she shook her head. "The bread man just left."

"You reduced the order?"

Tess nodded. "He looked disappointed, especially when I told him we were baking our own now."

"Don't worry." Claire poured herself a cup of coffee at the stove and refilled Tess's cup. "He'll be here early for lunch one day, now he knows that. How'd you do this morning?"

"The painting's done in the downstairs bathroom. The cold tap needs a new washer." Tess added a generous serving of cream to her coffee.

As Claire began to unload the dishwasher, Tess joined her, inverting clean glasses on a tray. When it was full, Claire carried it through the swinging door to the dining room. There was a series of tiny clinks as she stored the glasses in a hutch.

"Well! What do you know!" her surprised exclamation reached Tess distantly as she stacked clean plates on shelves beside the stove. She was about to call out when she heard the low sound of a deep voice answering Claire's. She was still on her knees when the door swung open slowly to reveal Evan's face.

He had pulled off his knitted cap and his tawny hair was slightly awry. The smooth prominence of his cheekbones formed handsome planes above the dark beard. Her heart seized as she looked at him, reckoning with how strongly beautiful his face was—how its facets always made him look just a bit different than she remembered him.

He dallied in the doorway, as though awaiting permission. His gaze swept the room as though he'd never seen it before.

Tess struggled to her feet. "Been a while, has it?"

He nodded slowly. "Yes, quite a while. I thought I might have a look at the ballroom, if you still want me to."

The ballroom had been her biggest project so far and his timing was remarkable. She'd just finished painting its walls and ceiling days before. The sconces were repaired and polished, the piano tuned. Only the floor remained, and she'd been sure he'd forgotten about it. This stirred a curious war inside her—disappointment battling relief.

In the days since her discoveries at the library, Tess had fled from thoughts of him because no matter how hard she tried she couldn't seem to bring her most recent visit with him into focus. It was all overshadowed by the confusing implications of what she'd read in those newspaper stories.

Things were never what they seemed. Better not to count on anything. Just like with Andy. Even the hours she spent trying to upgrade the Spinnaker offered no escape from what her mind still slipped back to.

Claire shooed Evan from where he was still standing in the doorway. "Come in, for goodness sake." She looked at him. "Ballroom, huh?" She waved a hand dismissively. "Empty stomach's more likely."

A grin replaced his uncertain expression. He laughed in earnest when she motioned him into a chair at the table, set a canister of cookies before him, and quickly added a mug of coffee.

"Only to please you, Claire. You know me so well." He helped himself to an enormous chocolate chip cookie.

Tess watched them silently.

"Reverse psychology," Claire told her. "He spent years getting underfoot in this kitchen, and no cookie is safe from him." Her eyes were very bright as they turned to him. "You're not a moment too soon. The place is falling apart and it'll be a miracle if this poor girl stays in Knowle after the time she's had trying to keep up. It was all I could do to keep her from tackling that floor herself."

"Still the same." His aqua eyes twinkled at Tess. "Next she'll show me where I tracked in mud last time!"

"Can't remember when that was." Claire fixed her gaze on him. "Don't you be setting foot in here, Evan Marston, 'less you plan to make it regular. I'm getting too old for comings and goings I can't count on."

His features softened as he chewed slowly.

Tess understood then that Evan hadn't been here since his fall. One look at his face, and Claire's, made it plain that this little exchange was as charged with emotional reunion as any embrace would be, that they had both missed this very much.

"You're still a great cook," he said.

"Ah, but Tess is the baker, these days."

Tess felt she had been watching something very old and very personal, and hadn't wanted to intrude by speaking. What she did want, she knew with certainty now, was to make him feel as welcome here as Claire was trying to do, help cast off whatever ghosts had kept him away.

He turned to her. "Shall we go have a look?"

As she led him the long way through the front hall, Evan ambled slowly behind, glancing around him as they approached the back of the Inn. "You've been very busy here. The Tasker House is going to pale by comparison."

Cold air surrounded them when Tess opened the ballroom's double doors. The room seemed instantly warmer when she turned on the four brass and crystal chandeliers overhead. She found another switch and light from the wall sconces showed the results of her work. To suit the room's period architecture, she'd painted its walls soft mauve and chosen a gleaming ivory shade for the woodwork. The details around the light fixtures on the ceiling had been a particular challenge and her neck was still sore from the effort.

Evan whistled softly as he strode around taking it in. "I've remembered this as such a dark room."

"It was," she agreed as she huddled into her heavy sweater. "Even with all those tall windows."

Evan looked out at the street through one of them. "Now it's an especially beautiful place to watch the sun set." He turned and began pacing, absorbed in some exercise of measurement. "The floor's not bad, actually. But I'm afraid this nice new paint will get awfully dusty from the sanding."

Tess shrugged. "I figured it was better to leave this until last. There was no way to get all that other work done without compromising a new floor." She was hugging herself tightly to keep from shivering and her voice was starting to quaver.

"Go get warm," he urged. "I'll just look around here a little more."

She nodded gratefully and shot through the doors.

It wasn't just that she was cold. The big room was chilly, but her teeth hadn't chattered like this in all the time she'd worked in there, wearing far lighter clothes.

This was the effort of containing her response when he spoke to her, looked at her—especially when he looked at her. Like she had swallowed a feather, as though he could see everything inside her.

The kitchen was empty and she stood close to the woodstove. Gradually the shivering ceased, became a flush of excitement. He would come here, after all. Wasn't that part of what had pushed her so hard these past weeks? More than expending her restless energy, filling the unpleasant void winter had brought, hadn't she been working to have her vision complete before him when he came? Offer him something new, something hers?

His footsteps sounded behind her and she turned quickly.

He went to the table to drain the last of his coffee then began buttoning his coat.

"You won't have to work in that cold," Tess said. "We'll turn up the heat."

"No need to run up bills. A space heater will do fine. I'll bring one with me. But I probably can't get to it till the first of the year. Maybe you don't want to wait that long."

"Oh, that'll be fine," she said. "Why don't you figure out an estimate?"

"For the work?" he asked. "Oh, I don't want to be paid for that."

Her eyes widened in surprise.

"You can feed me," he decided. "By the time I'm finished, you'll have paid for your floor twice over!"

"Surely, that's not enough. We'll pay for the supplies, at least."

"I've got most of what I'll need." His expression reassured her. "I'd like to do this, as long as you don't mind me taking my time. I have to fit it between some things."

Mind? The thought of regular contact, having him here for a span that was indefinite, seemed the brightest hope she'd felt since buying the Spinnaker.

"No, not at all," she said.

"Very good. Then I'll be in touch."

"Thank you for coming, Evan."

Thank you for being here, her thoughts added as the door closed behind him.

Chapter 5

Beyond the glimpse she caught of him as he left Dickie's Store one afternoon, Tess didn't see Evan again as December's holiday weeks arrived. Her mother spent Christmas in Knowle and the three women passed the hours inside together when frigid temperatures and battering winds made going out unbearable.

Pearl brought lots of good ideas for the Inn, and surprised Tess by suggesting she swap her car for the vintage Mercedes her mother had driven north. "Helmut," whose name emblazoned his license plate, had come home with her parents from Germany twenty years earlier. After Tess's father died, the car was extra precious to Pearl, yet she insisted her wintry commutes would be safer in the Toyota Tess hardly drove now.

"It will help you feel close to Dad," she coaxed. "He wants to help you."

So, here it was, the real reason for this plan. Tess wondered how any car, even a well-loved one, could be the means of otherworldly help and communication.

At loose ends the day Pearl left, she received a call from Rowan inviting her to dinner for New Year's Eve and her spirits were instantly buoyed. The last day of the year was cold but sunny. It was already pitch black outside when Tess pulled on her coat as the Inn's kitchen clock struck six.

Claire was elbow-deep in a baking project. "Take my car, if you like."

Helmut's starter had died that morning, perhaps in protest of his new surroundings, or the extreme cold. When Tess tried to imagine what sort of disembodied "communication" this might represent, all she could hear was the only expression of anger her pragmatic father ever allowed himself: "Fiddlesticks!" She pictured Helmut sulking where he sat in Harve Cooper's garage awaiting the new part.

"Oh, no, thanks," she said. "I'm kind of looking forward to the walk."

"It's supposed to start storming around midnight." Claire's head was bent over the pie crust she was rolling out. "I suppose Evan can give you a ride home." She lifted the dough carefully into pie plates.

Tess stared at her.

"Uh, oh." Claire's expression was contrite. "Don't you know about that?"

Confusion crossed Tess's features. "About what?"

"Oh, Claire," the other woman chided herself. "You've gone and let a cat out again. I heard Dickie asking Evan about his plans for New Year's when he came into the store yesterday. Seems he received the same invitation you did. Knowing Rowan, I bet you prove just as big a surprise to Evan as he obviously has to you." Claire's mouth worked into a fond smile. "That old rascal."

Tess tugged her boots on near the back door. "Well—" She glanced at the clock and drew a deep breath. "Guess I'd better go."

"Sure you don't want the car?"

Tess paused, hand on the knob of the back door. "No, I'm glad to walk." She really needed it now.

"Have fun! See you—"

"... next year," Tess finished with her, the words forming small clouds as she stepped out into the cold air.

She hurried along the empty sidewalks. The moon was a smear of white behind the cloud cover of the impending storm, and the light from Rowan's house was a beacon across the harbor, where the tide had risen high. Tess tucked her chin deep into her muffler, away from the nip of the wind off the water.

Her feet skidded on an unseen patch of ice as she approached the house. Then she spied the Volvo wagon backed close to the door. She paused for a few seconds before she rapped firmly on the door. When she heard the sounds of voices on the other side, she realized she had come to the front door where she usually let herself in the back. Something tonight made her feel more like a visitor than a regular.

She was bathed in a wash of light and warmth as the door

creaked open. The figure in the doorway was a shadow in the light behind it, but the deep resonance was unmistakable in the voice that urged, "Come in, Tess."

She finally saw Evan's face as she crossed the threshold. A dimple was visible as he smiled at her, and she was surprised to see that no beard now framed the upturned corners of his mouth.

Cooking aromas had filled the house. "Something sure smells good," she said as she drew them in.

"Let's hope it'll live up to its promise. May I take your coat?"

She thanked him as she slid out of it and handed him her hat and scarf. She caught sight of herself in the hall mirror and saw the walk had turned her cheeks pink.

"Ah, you've met the chef then." Rowan's face creased in a smile as he moved toward her leaning on a cane. His cap of white hair shone and a tie and tweed jacket had replaced his customary cardigan and plaid wool shirt. "We're having one of Evan's masterpieces tonight. He makes a superlative chowder, you know."

"Well, Rowan, you've planned all sorts of surprises." Tess glanced up at Evan, who raised his hand to mask a growing smile.

"Surprises seem to be Rowan's biggest masterpieces," he told her, then moved toward the swinging door to the kitchen and held it open. "Shall we?"

"Sounds capital to me." Rowan gestured Tess through ahead of him.

"How can I help?"

"Be a good guest and have a seat," Evan said.

Rowan joined Tess at the table as Evan placed heaping bowlfuls of chowder and a plate of warm cornbread in front of them. He filled their glasses with cider, then disappeared into the next room. Soft piano sounds drifted in behind him from the stereo when he returned and seated himself across from her.

Rowan took the plate of cornbread from Tess and told her, "This particular meal has become rather a tradition for Evan and me."

"Thanks for including me." She sampled the chowder then said, "This really is wonderful, Evan."

The buttery broth was creamy, thick with potatoes and several kinds of fish, as well as shrimp and tender scallops.

He set a dish of pickles near her place as he thanked her.

"Old, carefully-guarded recipe?"

"No. Just thrown together in the same distracted way my father did."

"Oh, and did he!" Rowan smacked his lips at the memory.

For several minutes their spoons made the only sounds, along with the ice that clinked like wind chimes in the glasses they raised.

Rowan set his spoon down and stared thoughtfully out the window. "Here we're catching our breath between blizzards and Dickie's making plans for his garden."

Evan rolled his eyes. "He tried to unload some of his turkeys on me last week."

"For your freezer?" Tess asked.

"Oh no," he said. "These are the kind you have to feed."

"With or without jackets?" Rowan wondered with a small smile.

Evan erupted in a deep laugh. "I should have asked him that."

Rowan saw the confusion on Tess's face. "I take it Tess hasn't heard the story?"

"Not if she's lucky."

"Aw, go ahead. It's been years since I've heard you tell it."

Tess raised her brows at him encouragingly as she finished her mouthful.

Evan took a breath and began, "My father thought if you owned property, you were obliged to grow something on it." He dabbed at his freshly-shaven chin. "Every year, we'd have a sort of half-hearted garden, which neither of us really wanted to care for. It managed to thrive on neglect anyway. The squashes did, anyhow."

He noticed that she'd finished her chowder and rose to offer her more.

"Not just yet," she told him. "Please go on."

He settled back in his chair. "I was probably about ten when he got himself a couple of turkeys. The noise level around the place increased, as you can probably imagine. And Dad felt a little more like a farmer."

His listeners smiled as he continued, "One day he got called away before he'd had a chance to feed and water them. He always did it himself and didn't want to relinquish the responsibility, but Dickie was with me and talked him into letting us handle it.

"After he left, we got a bucket of feed, then found a steel pail of water like the one I'd seen him use and took that out too. We got the job done in no time and felt pretty proud of ourselves. What we didn't know was that the contents of that pail was some sort of homemade gin Dickie's father, Gil, who fancied himself kind of a brew master, had sent over. Dad didn't drink and planned to ditch it when he got a chance.

"After a while, those turkeys quieted right down."

"I'll bet!" Tess laughed quickly and both men joined her.

"We figured we'd done a good job. Then a little later, we looked out to see them careening around the yard."

Laughter escaped both Evan and his listeners as he demonstrated for them with his head. "Then they started to fall over—kind of like statues."

He paused to take a swallow of his cider. "We were terrified. Certain those turkeys were dying right before our eyes as the result of what we'd done. Neither of us knew what to do, then Dickie remembered that they'd had to pluck the birds his father raised. He convinced me that we could at least get that job out of the way, then maybe the news wouldn't sit so hard with my dad."

"Oh, no!" Tess cried as Rowan chuckled.

Nodding, Evan continued, "We diligently relieved those birds of about half their feathers. Then my father came home and they started to come round. Dickie considered it a miracle but the poor birds were miserable. And I felt awful. Dad had the vet come over to take a look. Maudey—Dickie's mother—was furious when she heard. Once she'd finished reaming out his father, she whipped up some little red flannel jackets, which those birds wore until their demise a few months later."

"What an experience!" Tess said.

"I promise never to talk about it when turkey's on the menu." He reached for their empty bowls. "I hope I haven't spoiled your appetites. Shall we have some more?"

They nodded eagerly.

"Few things seemed to trouble your father," Rowan observed.

"I suppose not," Evan said. "I think raising me took a year or two off his life, though."

Their discussion shifted toward news of Rowan's family, and Tess's plans for the Spinnaker. Evan suggested they wait for dessert and coffee. Tess began clearing dishes to the sink.

"Oh, leave them," Rowan said.

"They won't take long," she said and quickly set to work.

Evan raised his fists in a stretch then vigorously massaged his left leg, which he had stretched on a spare chair.

Rowan frowned at him across the table. "See? You pushed yourself to finish painting that ceiling and now you probably won't sleep."

Evan shrugged. "Something's going to make it ache anyhow."

Rowan got up and moved off toward his studio. After a few moments, Tess noticed that Evan hadn't followed, but was reaching for a towel in the rack beside her.

They exchanged smiles as he began dismantling what she had heaped in the drainer. The clatter of plates and swish of water were the only sounds as he moved from drainer to sink, putting things away with easy familiarity, his limp more marked.

"I seem to see you about once a season," he said, finally. "I'm glad we have so many of them."

Her cheeks grew warm. "Do you come over here often?"

"As often as I can." She felt a dizzying rush as his gaze met her eyes. A smile worked at the corners of his mouth. "How about you?"

She shook her head regretfully. "I used to get over every couple of days but the past few weeks just got too full."

"That must mean you're getting lots done." He was filing silverware into the appropriate slots in a drawer.

"Actually, that work has come to a standstill with the holidays."

"Lots of guests?"

"Yeah, things were buzzing. Claire calls it summer in December. The amount of sand they track in from the parking lot makes it look that way, too."

The lines beside his mouth deepened as he smiled. "Do you share the cooking?"

"We try to take turns. I usually do breakfast. I worked an evening schedule for years and still need some incentive to get up in the morning." She squeezed out a sponge and wiped down the counter. "I'm going to dream about omelets for weeks."

She looked at him. "I don't suppose you'd have any interest in playing chef?"

"What, at the Spinnaker?" His brows raised in surprise. "I think Claire would throw me out if I as much as lifted a spatula there. She's a little too familiar with my—ah, checkered past. I helped with cooking there one summer." He shook his head. "Real mixed reviews."

Tess gestured toward the chowder on the stove. "She doesn't know what we're missing now."

"I'm afraid that somewhat irresponsible summer was enough to prejudice her against the idea for good, no matter how much my skills may have improved. Or are you doing the hiring these days?"

"Oh, no. I respect her judgment too much to take that away." She pulled the plug and watched the water swirl away.

"Maybe I'll redeem myself with her when I start that floor."

Tess turned to face him. "Oh, she's so happy you're coming, Evan. And I don't think the floor has anything to do with it."

He smiled broadly. "Wait till she figures out I'm just trying to get in the new innkeeper's good graces."

Tess blinked uncertainly.

His levity disappeared as he set the towel down and reached for her arm, aqua eyes insistent.

Her thoughts were scattered by the gentle pressure on her arm. A warm current flashed there, terminating somewhere short of her knees.

"Are you?" she asked softly.

He withdrew his hand and braced it on the counter beside him. His gaze dropped there too. "I guess maybe I am."

She was conscious of that odd current she'd felt when he'd touched her. It still seemed to lurk near the surface of her skin.

"She'd have the good sense to tell you you're wasting your time."

His expression was guarded.

She reached up and touched his cheek briefly. "There's no need to try for what you already have."

His uncertain expression, which had stiffened the planes of his face, dissolved in happiness then. It radiated from his eyes, danced at the corners of his mouth, shaping the sculpted contours of his face into more beauty than she thought she could bear.

"Are you two going to stay in there all night?" Rowan's voice called from the next room.

Conscious of the racing of her heart and the pulse of its beat in her ears, Tess took a step backward and pushed a cabinet door shut. "Looks like we're all set here, huh?"

Evan nodded and gestured her through to the studio ahead of

him.

Rowan was seated in his customary chair with a very pleased expression on his face. His completed portrait of her was displayed on an easel facing the door. "You see? A bit tardy, but a holiday present nonetheless."

With a small cry of delight, Tess moved to hug him, then turned to the painting.

Though it felt a little strange, it also felt right, this image of her looking back with pale skin and the satiny sheen of what he called her cola-colored hair.

"Rowan!" she breathed. "This is—well, I think it's much lovelier than it ought to be!"

Evan watched her from where he leaned against the door jamb. "I was the most faithless sitter, too," she told him.

"I had some wonderful photographs to work from," Rowan said.

"What he'll never tell you," Evan advised as he approached the portrait, "is that his best work is actually done from memory." His fingers reached out and traced the hairline of the face on the canvas. "You expect this to feel as much like silk as it looks."

"It's all just capturing what the light shows you," Rowan said. "If I waited until I thought it was finished, you would never have it. Evan convinced me that it was, and is going to help you get it home."

Tess beamed at both of them. "Thank you, Rowan."

A little later, she got a fire going in the fireplace while Evan made coffee. Soon the flames roared high, reddening their faces as they sat before them and talked long past midnight.

Then Evan and Tess thanked their host, bundled up against the cold, and hurried out to Evan's car. He let it coast down the driveway's incline until it started fitfully.

Light sleet was falling. They were quiet during the short ride to the Inn, where he pulled up near the kitchen door.

"I'll carry it," he said as he headed toward the back of the car to fetch the portrait where he'd packed it carefully.

Tess held the kitchen door open for him and he gently lowered the canvas onto the chair she indicated.

"What a delightful evening. Thank you so much for everything," she said.

In the pale light of the small lamp Claire had left on for her, he looked at her, nodding, but said nothing.

"You're welcome to stay for a while, if you like." She began to unwind the muffler from around her neck.

He gestured toward the sound of the Volvo's engine idling. "The roads are starting to slick up, so I'd better get home."

Then he hesitated, mouth twisting thoughtfully. "I'll be by soon to start that floor."

"That'll be great. Be careful out there."

"Always." His smile was ironic as he fit his knitted cap over his hair then leaned toward her almost imperceptibly. "Good night, Tess."

On impulse, she caught hold of his free hand and reached to place a kiss on the generous plane of his cheek, which was very cold. "Thank you, Evan."

With a look of surprise, he let both his arms circle her loosely, then pressed his face against her hair almost tentatively.

"Happy New Year." The voice near her ear was low.

His breath was warm as their features drifted together, and then he pressed his lips to her forehead decisively and was gone.

Happily exhausted, she crossed the room to switch off the lamp before she climbed the stairs.

It was when she paused for one last look at her portrait that she noticed the small cardboard box beside it on the chair. Its only embellishment was her name in precise block caps.

She gasped with delighted recognition when she pulled back the flaps of the box and saw what was inside. Removing it carefully, she cradled the miniature Spinnaker in her palm and explored its intricately detailed surface with trembling fingers. He had left the two halves loosely joined so she would discover that it had utility as well as beauty. The smell of cedar wafted out as she separated them.

Fitting the box together again, she released a happy sigh and sank into a chair. No wonder he'd seemed in such a hurry. There was probably no other way he could manage something like this. Such an enigma he was, so direct in some ways, so reticent in others.

Throughout the evening, she'd found herself wondering about so many things. How much did he think about Celia? What had he been like before fate had cut so deeply into his life, as it had into her own? Were there just too many things she would never be able to know about him?

Yet how nice it had been, too, to watch his ease in a place where he obviously felt so very much at home.

Tess held his gift in her lap, turning it over in her hands as her vision clouded with tears. With complete clarity, she recalled what she had sensed from him on that summer day by the shore. The tears felt burning hot as they trickled down her cheeks. The doubts and questions she had harbored about him since were powerless in the waves of love and remorse that surged in her now.

When a patient named Andy Hollinger had died unexpectedly under Tess's care, she had been blameless in everyone's eyes but her own, because Andy had become the center of her universe. But despite the heavy sentence she'd imposed on herself in an agony of unbelieving grief, she had never had to face the kind of ugly suspicion that shrouded Evan's pain, even though she knew she was accountable, that she was at fault.

When Pearl had heard the news of Evan's accident that summer, she had seemed to know the truth of that matter—had known in the inexplicable way she often knew about things the mind can't grasp all on its own. Her mother had sensed immediately—and declared assertively—that Evan was blameless, and that he would suffer for it just the same.

Use your heart's ears, Pearl always told her. *Listen to hear from the inside of someone and you'll learn what the true story is.*

Evan's story and trust had been plain in his eyes from the start, shown to her freely, but she had been blind, undeserving of it. Now he offered it still, and she couldn't remember a gift that seemed as precious.

She wiped at her cheeks with the back of her hand. It was love and safety that had drawn her to the Spinnaker. Surely these could draw him back, too.

Chapter 6

Evan chose to have neither a phone nor a computer when he returned to Knowle after his accident and isolated himself. Though he'd recently acquired a land line, Tess wasn't able to get through when she called to thank him.

The sleet that had kept him from staying turned into a storm that dropped nearly two feet of snow and knocked out power, immobilizing the Village for days.

The smell of cinnamon pervaded the Inn's kitchen as Tess pressed her forehead against the glass of the back door. She watched the progress of the first delivery van to finally get through as it made its cautious way out of the Inn's parking lot.

"Driving look any better?" Claire asked as she set two mugs of coffee on the table alongside the sweet rolls Tess had baked that morning.

"Looks atrocious, but at least it's possible."

Claire settled at the table with a pleased expression. "How did I manage to forget to have breakfast?"

"Too much else to think about, I guess," Tess shrugged and took a seat across from her.

"Now what have I had to think about? Place could run itself this week. I stopped counting customers when I kept falling asleep during those long intervals between them."

Tess smiled as she buttered a roll and chewed it appreciatively. "How was Rowan yesterday? Is he managing all right?"

"Happy as a clam, living on chili and eggs, and much too excited about a new canvas to be much use for conversation. I did have a nice chat with Evan, though." She cupped her hand near the edge of the table and herded crumbs into it. "I suggested that he come by here on his way home but he was in a hurry to get back to some project he needs to finish before the end of the week."

Tess's pulse quickened. She'd felt thwarted by the foul weather, her freedom hampered even further by Helmut's absence, though she doubted she'd have had the courage to venture out on the roads before this anyway. She couldn't imagine one more day of hanging around inside now that they were clear.

The older woman sucked bits of icing from her fingers.

"Claire, I really don't like to ask this … But would you mind if I used your car?"

"Not a bit, if you've got a hankering to dig it out." Her voice was sympathetic. "Harve may be good but he's never been speedy."

"I told him there was no hurry," Tess admitted.

Claire rolled her eyes. "There'll be robins roosting in it before you get it back. You take mine anytime you want. You don't have to ask."

Tess thanked her. "I can pick some things up at the IGA. Why don't you see what we need?"

As Tess donned her outer clothes, Claire reached into her over-sized black purse for the keys. Tess caught them nimbly when she tossed them across the room.

The little red Honda was soon idling loudly as Tess shoveled off the mountain of snow that nearly obscured it from view. Her exertion had her well warmed up by the time she ducked back into the Inn.

"Been just like a caged animal waiting for this chance, haven't you?" Claire's hazel eyes twinkled a golden brown. "Think you can remember how to find his place?"

Tess smiled sheepishly under Claire's knowing gaze. "As a matter of fact, I just realized that the only route I know isn't going to be very accessible right now!"

"His driveway may not be a whole lot better, even if he's managed to get out. Be sure to stay in his tracks."

Tess listened to her directions carefully, drained her coffee, then headed outside.

She never shifted out of second gear, the going was so slow, and her heart quivered each time she felt the tires slip. The car quickly threw out an excess of heat and she loosened her coat as she crept along through mountainous snow banks. Many of the landmarks

Claire had given were buried now and she had to watch carefully.

Snow Fence Road wasn't nearly as clear as the streets in the village but its surface was well-packed. Eventually, she spied the red mailbox Claire had told her to look for and turned slowly into the drive. She was thankful to find it plowed.

The track was heavily wooded on both sides. Tree branches weighed down by snowfall hung low overhead, scraping the roof of the car in some spots.

She finally saw the weathered shingles of the house when she reached a small clearing. The patch of ocean visible beyond it was a steely color. The Volvo's grille faced her as she braked in front of the house. She noted with relief that whoever had plowed the drive had left enough space in which to turn the car around and did so before she parked and got out.

The house faced the ocean, and wind off the water knifed through her as she hurried to the front door and knocked. After several tries, she turned the knob and peered inside.

"Evan? Hello?" Her voice echoed off a cathedral ceiling with wide beams over the big L-shaped space that contained kitchen and living area.

There was no response.

She stepped inside and shut the door on the gusting wind.

The woodstove was built up on a slate platform set on the wide pine floorboards. She moved closer to hold her gloved hands near its heat.

One door off the room led into a small greenhouse that hugged the south side of the house. Tess stepped carefully around the space heater that stood at its entrance and looked in. It was nearly as warm as the bigger room it adjoined. A pile of small logs was stacked against the outside wall.

She wandered toward the two rooms at the back and studied the hand-turned doors admiringly. Everything was made of wood, even the latch handles, which he had surely made himself.

Two paintings that she recognized as Rowan's style were hung on the wall between them. One was a familiar view of the harbor; the other showed Moorish-looking buildings, perhaps in Spain.

The door on her left opened into a workroom where boards of varying lengths were stored on racks and shelves that lined the walls. A well-worn photograph of the Spinnaker rested against the back of the workbench. Tess remembered Evan's gift with a rush of affection.

She took off her gloves and explored the newly sanded smoothness of a table in the center of the room. A tall, narrow cabinet nearby contained dozens of small drawers, each with a hand-drawn illustration of the screw or fitment stored inside it. One wall was a giant pegboard hung with tools. The room seemed spacious, even with the large table saw in the corner and she smiled as she realized that this would be the master bedroom in most houses. Sawdust on the floor had been swept into small, neat piles.

She hesitated on the threshold of the other room whose door was only halfway ajar. A press bench was tucked against the wall, just inside it, and the weights resting at the top were icy cold when she laid her hand on them. A faded afghan was folded at the foot of the large bed and a dark-blue comforter was spread out on top. Books filled the shelves in the headboard that, she supposed, was also Evan's handiwork.

There was less daylight here than in the workroom, but the light from its west-facing windows had a magical effect on the small painting over the bed, the only interruption in the otherwise stark expanse of white plaster.

The winter sunset it depicted in fine detail seemed to glow, its exacting blend of corals and purples appearing to shift subtly before her eyes, as though a tiny window had opened on an actual animated scene.

Tess lost all sense of intruding as she moved toward it. The scene in the painting had a familiar quality and on closer inspection, she realized that she had seen it, numerous times in fact, especially in the last few months. It was the view from one of the tall windows in the Spinnaker's ballroom.

A fleeting recollection passed through her mind, of Evan's words as he'd stood before it: "Now it's an especially beautiful place to watch the sun set."

The varnished grain of the ballroom window's ledge in the foreground of the painting was captured so precisely that her fingers reached out to it automatically, as Evan's had to Rowan's canvas of her portrait. Beyond the painting's window were uneven rooftops, the crooked chimney of the parsonage with the rounded cap of the church steeple right behind it, and a snowy expanse of fields and pine forest that rose to meet the sky. Close up, the sunset's palette was even more vibrant—clouds of color melding into each other.

Rowan's work never showed the photographic quality of this painstaking realism. The brush strokes were barely visible as she scanned for some indication of the artist. All she found was a character, like oriental script, tucked beneath the window's ledge.

She released her breath slowly as she remembered her surroundings. It was as though the world had stood still during these last moments. She wandered toward the kitchen. Perhaps she'd find paper and leave a note.

Some sort of automobile-engine part had been set on a bed of newspaper in the middle of the kitchen's big oak table. Tess turned toward the furniture assembled around the woodstove. The surface of a small table near the couch was covered with reading material. The book of Rilke's she'd found for Rowan lay face-down on top of one about building wooden sailboats. She lifted the cover of a large sketch pad full of conceptual drawings of furniture and flipped through it slowly.

A sound of distant crunching startled her—like that of tires on packed snow. She hurried toward the door, not wanting to be discovered inside like a trespasser.

Wind was whipping the snow around and it collected quickly on the dark wool of her sleeve. She bolted toward Claire's car and had nearly reached it when she trod hard on something. There was no traction on the ice as she struggled to regain her balance. A sound tore out of her as her hands flew out too late and her head hit the ground.

Tears smarted in her eyes as she gasped in cold air. Why hadn't she paid more attention? A vise of pain yanked her back down when she tried to raise her head, and her confused thoughts were just turning to fearful worry when darkness overcame them.

•

Dickie Foster's father, Gil, hadn't seen Evan for several months and looked like he'd seen a ghost when he opened the door and found him there.

Maude Foster insisted he stay for some of the Brunswick stew she'd just made, especially after his long walk. A mile and a half wasn't "neighbors" in everybody's book.

Unfortunately, Gil wasn't able to help him out with the tools he'd come for.

"Dickie must have them with him in the van. I know they ain't here anywheres."

The words escaped sideways around the pipe clenched in Gil's teeth. "Funny, you havin' that fancy European car and not getting some of your own, ain't it?" He lifted his cap and began to scratch his spikey gray crewcut noisily.

"Oh, I did." Evan's mouth tugged upwards at Gil's description of the Volvo, which Dickie always assured him kept the manufacturers of Bondo in business.

The head scratching became a stroking motion as Gil watched him, confused.

"They're with Dickie," Evan finished simply with a shrug.

"Oh, Jesum, I'm sorry," Gil's face colored quickly as he replaced the cap. "I'll be sure and tell 'im to get 'em right back to ya." His tone meant business.

Evan thanked him as he suppressed a smile holding back too much laughter.

"I got a Toyota myself, of course," Gil went on, "but I don't do much on it." He struck a match against the side of the iron stove.

The flame made a loud hiss and Maude shot him a look of disapproval.

Evan dabbed at his mouth and started to rise from the table.

"I take mine into Harve's instead. This morning he was working on one of them—what you call it? Mercedes Bends." Gil's diction turned the name into a verb. His cheeks puffed hugely as the match's torchlike flame ignited his tobacco. "Never did bother getting myself any of them funny metric wrenches and such."

Evan intercepted Maude at the stove as she was preparing to ladle more stew into his bowl. "That was plenty Maudey. Thanks a lot."

"I bet you don't eat half right on your own out there. Have a little more."

"Any more and I'll be too full to walk home!" His leg ached so much now it wouldn't be easy going anyway. "Thank you both." He dove quickly toward his coat. "Tell Dickie I'll be in touch, okay?"

"Let me drop you home." Gil reached for his own jacket. "I got some things to do in town. I'll get your tools and drop 'em off on my way home."

"That'd be great, Gil, thanks." Evan followed him to his pick-up.

So much for a quick trip to the Foster's for his tools. As they jounced down the drive, clouds of Gil's cherry tobacco smoke swirled around them.

Absolutely nothing had worked out so far today. He had cracked a perfectly good piece of wood through sheer stupidity. He'd been in a fog all morning, though he'd slept like a stone through most of the night. Maybe that was why. Probably wasn't used to it.

He'd been all set to go into town when he'd discovered the puddle under the engine after the Volvo didn't start. "Probably time to retire you soon," he'd muttered as he explored under the hood. He had a spare fuel pump, luckily, but then remembered that Dickie had his tools. On impulse, he'd decided to walk over to the Fosters'.

They'd passed no other traffic by the time Gil reached the foot of Evan's drive.

"That's some mailbox you got there," he noted. "Big. Red. No way the mailman can miss that."

"Unfortunately, neither does the plow," Evan said. He had painted it a brilliant vermilion that matched the snow fences but the plow had still knocked it over twice.

"Want me to take you all the way in?"

"No, thanks a lot, Gil. This is fine."

A single set of tire tracks was faintly visible in the increasing whiteness of the dirt track. Anticipation swelled uneasily inside him.

A sound, almost a cry, startled his ears when he reached the clearing behind the house. His dragging footsteps quickened as he rounded the building. He stopped short when he caught sight of the red Honda and the inert form on the ground beside it.

His gut wrenched with fear as he bolted forward and saw the bright blood in the snow beside Tess's face.

Splinting his left knee, he eased down alongside her and touched her limbs carefully. Relief washed through him when he heard the soft moan in her throat as her head moved slightly.

He pulled her against him, locking his teeth at the fire that blazed in his leg when he raised them both. He hurried to the door, scolding her carelessness softly, gratefully.

Inside, he lowered her onto the couch. As he folded a pillow under her head, his hand found the sticky patch on the right side. He pulled it away, bloodied, and she twitched violently as he inadvertently brushed the large lump that had formed there.

He went to his bedroom and returned with the afghan and another blanket, both of which he wrapped around her. He filled a basin with warm water at the sink and found ice, towels, some clean rags and a pair of scissors.

"I'm back," he told her hopefully as he neared the couch, then sighed at her unresponsiveness. He set the things down and raised her head higher with another pillow. Slowly, he cleaned the tacky blood from her hair, cutting away several dark locks.

She stiffened, wincing with the effort to open her eyes. Finally her lids lifted and she eyed him glassily. She tried to sit up, then dropped back with a groan.

"Lie still now, Tess," he whispered. "You've had a hell of a fall."

•

Sometime later, Tess opened her eyes and immediately felt the sensation of her head spinning. She touched the throbbing place on her head, trying to piece events together. Evan's back was to her as he rapidly tossed wood into the stove.

His eyes were kind when they met hers. He reached and lightly placed one hand under her chin, the other on her crown, as he turned her head toward him.

"I feel soooo stupid," she said.

"Just lie quiet now till I see to this."

He wrapped ice in a towel and held it against her head.

"I can do that." She reached groggily to find it.

He brought the basin to the sink and returned with a flashlight. "That's a prizewinner you've got there. I'm worried you may have a concussion."

He shone the flashlight in each of her eyes, then seemed relieved. "I think you're okay. Let's get that dressed, then you can hold the ice against it."

Evan cut two long strips from the rags, folding one in several layers. He placed it over the wound and wrapped the other around her head several times, securing it over her left ear with a small knot. After he wrapped fresh ice in a dry towel, he laid it against her head and surveyed his handiwork. "Almost stylish," he said with a wry smile. "And about the extent of my first-aid abilities."

He still wore his navy pea coat and knitted watch cap.

"Seaman Marston to the rescue." She looked at him gratefully. "I'm so sorry to put you to all this trouble. Won't you take your coat off and stay a while?"

He snatched off his cap with a self-conscious grin as he reached to unbutton his coat, then rose to clear the supplies away to the kitchen. He had left the door of the woodstove open and its heat began to penetrate the layers heaped on top of her.

"Here, let's get your coat off." He pulled the blankets back and helped her to a sitting position. He slid her jacket off her shoulders and she groaned as a sickening wave of dizziness overtook her.

"Still spinning?" He eased her back down. "I don't know whether it's better to keep you still or try to get you back home."

"Let's just go with your first choice for now. It's getting better, really."

He regarded her doubtfully then wondered with a smile, "May I ask what you were doing?"

"I was trying to get back to Claire's car so it wouldn't look like I'd been snooping around in here."

"Had you?"

She nodded sheepishly then winced. "Serves me right for trespassing. I just wanted to thank you for the wonderful little surprise you left behind the other night."

"Oh. Did you like that?"

"I much more than liked it, Evan."

"Well. Good." His smile seemed pleased as he turned toward the stove.

She snuggled under the blankets contentedly, remembering the scent of him, like hay and soap, as he'd leaned over her. A flush crept over her as she thought of how cool the back of his hand had been when it brushed her cheek.

She gazed across at where he hunkered now, fussing with the woodstove.

"Fool thing never works half right." His face showed exasperation. "I either freeze or I cook." He reached down and pulled his heavy wool sweater over his head. His strong, smooth neck was visible now, and his hair looked darker in this light, tendrils of it curling at the nape of his neck.

He turned toward her. "Well, it's nice to find you here, despite the circumstances."

"Yeah. Guess it was worth the trip." She covered her mouth at the unintended pun.

He shot her a look of surprise. His laugh joined hers and was renewed each time their eyes met.

"Still, I wish you hadn't gone jumping to contusions."

She uttered a groan and he wrinkled his nose in apologetic agreement.

"So, you had a look around my little cave?"

"Is that what you recluse types call it?"

"Actually, we prefer to be called hermits."

She nodded. "Yes, 'recluse' always sounds kind of wild. 'Hermit' seems homier, maybe because it makes me think of cookies."

He laughed softly.

"I did take a look around, since the door wasn't locked. It's very nice. Did you build it?"

"My dad did—got the shell finished before he died, anyway. Some of the woodwork inside is his too. He's the one who started my love affair with carpentry."

He caught his lower lip between his teeth thoughtfully. "It was the best possible inheritance, for me, that and this place. He spent his whole life working so hard. I don't know just what he got out of it."

"Oh, that's easy," Tess said quickly. "He had you. That's a job he did very well."

He cocked his head as though considering this, then moved toward the couch. Her heart felt larger as he placed a palm on either side of her and leaned close to meet her eyes. "He'd sure have liked you."

His gaze swept from her eyes to her throat before he retrieved the ice pack from where it had fallen away and laid it gently against her scalp. "Rest, now. I'm going to dig out my car and pray Gil Foster brings my tools before it gets too dark to work. It's not going anywhere without a new fuel pump."

She watched as he donned his coat and reached for the part on the table before disappearing outside. His shovel made a rhythmic scraping as he worked it. Soon, she closed her eyes and dozed.

•

Evan was nudging chunks of ice from the Volvo's wheels when Gil drove in. Smoke billowed as he rolled down his window and handed over the tools. "Need help?"

Evan had a quick urge to say yes, if only to watch his face. He knew Gil's mind was already on Maude's stew. The last thing he wanted was to help Evan wrestle with a fuel pump. "I should be all set. Thanks a lot, Gil."

"Looks like Claire Farragut's car over there." The older man gestured with the stem of his pipe. "You workin' on that, too?"

"Oh ... Tess—the new innkeeper. She, ah, drove it out."

Great, just great, Evan. Babble it right out, he chided himself, deciding not to elaborate further. A part of him still acted twelve years old around Dickie's father sometimes.

"Hmm." Gil's single word spoke volumes. "Well, good luck."

Evan waved to him as he turned his pick-up around and chugged out of the drive.

Well, the Village would buzz now.

The pump took much longer than he'd expected. After he got the Volvo started, he pulled it in front of Claire's car and hitched the two together with a tow chain. It was nearly dark when he finished, and his hands were frozen.

He had them clasped around a cup of tea when Tess opened her eyes a little later.

"How's the head?" Evan looked up quickly.

"Oh, not too bad." She struggled to sit up.

"Wait a minute now—don't rush things." He was on his feet and intercepted her as she moved crazily from side to side.

•

She tried to focus on the gyrating paleness of the refrigerator, willing the spinning to stop. "I'm trying to remember where I left the car keys," she said with a smile.

"Don't think for a minute you're driving anywhere."

"Maybe not. But I can't stay here all day. Or, night." She glanced out the window.

His face drew close to hers and the dizziness rallied as she sank back down.

Evan caught hold of her shoulders to help hold her upright. Then he dropped his hands to gather up her wrists before he perched on the couch beside her.

"Look at me," she said, her impatience rising. "If you got going again after what happened to you, I can certainly ..."

His features froze and he stood slowly as her voice trailed off.

She watched him wander away to the door in an uneven gait. "Oh, Evan—that was ... thoughtless. I'm very sorry."

He looked out through the glass and said nothing for several moments. When he spoke, his voice had deepened. "Just forget about it."

"I can't possibly understand how it was for you."

She saw a muscle tighten in his jaw.

"But I want to understand ..."

He shook his head.

"Please, Evan ..."

"No, Tess." His tone was firm. She didn't know how to break the ominous silence that followed. Finally he turned back toward her, his tone deliberately light. "We'd better get you back before Claire gets worried."

"What about your car?"

"It's all set." He shrugged his coat back on and reached for hers, brought it over, and held it as she found the sleeves clumsily. When she staggered uncertainly to her feet, he took her arm and guided her to the door.

The frigid air cleared her head quickly when she stepped outside.

"It might be better if you ride in the Honda, in case they separate," he said as he walked her toward it. "Do you feel up to it?"

Tess nodded and lowered herself into the driver's seat slowly. She put the stick shift in neutral as he instructed and was going to insist on driving herself but a sudden wave of vertigo made her think better of it.

"You all right?"

She nodded as the dizziness returned.

"I'll be right out. Just have to shut down the stove drafts." He closed the car door and went back inside. A few minutes later, he slid behind the wheel of the Volvo and soon had both cars crawling down the drive.

Tess switched on the hazard lights when Evan carefully negotiated the turn onto Snow Fence Road. Her head began a fresh pounding in the cold.

Her eyes watched the back of him as she pondered how she had broken the gentle camaraderie so senselessly. With just one small reference, everything about him had changed in an instant and the message was clear: This far, but no farther.

Chapter 7

Evan departed as soon as he'd delivered her into Claire's care. Depressed by the turn of events, Tess buried herself in what she could manage of the Inn's routine in the following days.

She was surprised when Harve Cooper phoned to say the work on Helmut was done and mentioned that Evan had stopped by the garage to check on his progress. When curiosity in Harve's voice grew thinly veiled, Tess ended the call on a businesslike note.

More guests filled the Inn during the next two weekends and she kept busy easily, though always with the hope that she'd turn to find Evan there. As days dragged into weeks and he didn't return, Tess grew more convinced of the gravity of her reference to his fall. A sense of self-doubt settled in, one as old as it was painful.

Her heart turned an especially big leap of excitement when she pulled Helmut into the Inn's parking lot after errands one day and saw Evan's car backed close to the kitchen entrance. When she shoved the back door open with bulky bags in her arms, a low hum was vibrating from the direction of the ballroom.

"Sander," Claire answered her questioning look loudly as she took the bags.

"Now this place really sounds like home!" Tess beamed. As she reached to unpack the bags Claire had set on the table, the other woman took the cans from her arms. "I'll get these. You go have a look."

Her heartbeat quickened as she moved nearer to the sander's deafening sound.

Evan's eyes turned toward her when she appeared on the ballroom's threshold. He lowered the mask that covered his nose and mouth and reached to shut off the machine. Its roar died slowly into silence.

"You thought I wasn't coming," he accused with a smile. Small particles of dust fell like snow in the beam of sunlight that turned his hair gold.

"What makes you think that?"

"Claire says you've booked a dance in two weeks!"

"Well, they didn't want to wait ..."

"They may find themselves dancing around patches of missing boards." At her distressed look, he quickly amended, "Of course, I'll see to it they don't."

She pressed a hand to her chest as she caught her breath. "That's enough time?"

"It'll be fine." His tone was confident, though her expression remained doubtful. "Don't look like that, Tess. I always tell the truth, especially about work."

"I—I wasn't sure what—your plans were," she stammered uncertainly.

"I told you what my plans were. Why would they change?"

"Sometimes ... things don't work out."

"They do when they're important enough." He regarded her evenly.

The next words wandered out, though she didn't want them to. "I wasn't sure. I thought, maybe, I'd put you off. When I—"

"Brought up something I didn't want to talk about?" he cut in quickly.

She nodded without looking at him.

He considered this, then said, "Well, I think that's my problem, Tess. Not yours."

His expression put her mind at rest.

She turned away to inspect his work and, in an instant, felt delicate movement lifting the hair on the side of her head.

"Not a trace of it now, is there?" His hand moved lightly over where the lump had risen angrily weeks before.

"Thanks to that competent doctor I had."

"I knew being a Boy Scout would pay off, sooner or later." His eyes sparked with sudden recollection as he scanned the room.

"Hey—come look at this." He gestured for her to follow as he ambled toward one of the tall windows. A section of the baseboard beneath it was missing.

"I took the liberty of removing this, since the piece was pretty badly gouged. Look what I found underneath." His finger underlined markings in the old plaster.

"It's a signature," Tess discovered as she studied the name, which had the year 1900 etched next to it.

"Workman must have put it there when he finished," Evan said. "I find these in older places every once in a while."

"Yes, my parents found a couple in a house they had near Rensselaer. Now we know how long it's been since someone took this off to paint it," Tess said. "Did you ever leave your name behind?"

"Oh, once or twice when I was younger. And more arrogant."

"Just think, years from now somebody will uncover it and wonder about you."

"More likely they'll just want to get the job over with and be glad they have better tools to do it!"

She laughed. "I won't keep you if you've got a deadline hanging over your head." She backed slowly toward the door. "Will you stay for dinner?"

"Not tonight, but I'll be here bright and early for breakfast, how's that?" His grin disappeared beneath the mask he fitted over the lower half of his face.

"Pancakes be all right?"

The eyes that widened in pleased assent were especially arresting all by themselves as the sander growled to life.

•

The sounds of his work became a welcome part of life at the Spinnaker and Tess went about her tasks happily aware of his presence. At night she lay awake remembering the warmth of Evan's company at mealtimes, the thoughtful expression he wore as he worked, his low, throaty laugh. She mentally compiled an ever-increasing list of mannerisms: the lines that quirked at the upturned corners of his mouth, the light that danced in his eyes, the large hands that fell with unconscious protectiveness over his left knee, or curled palm-upward on his thigh at rest.

He melded easily into the Inn's routine, finding little things to tend to beyond his work on the ballroom floor, even stepping into the rush at mealtimes and handling whatever task was one too many for Claire or Tess. They grew accustomed to having him a working part of their day before they all settled down to the meals that lingered long over the coffee that rounded them off. He'd been coming to the Spinnaker for about a week when he suddenly had a helper.

Matthew Crane was a dark-haired five-year-old with eyes like large chocolates in a face that, more often than not, bore a very serious expression. His parents had come to Knowle from Wisconsin and booked rooms at the Spinnaker while they awaited completion of the house that had been part of the promotion with which his father's company had lured them east. Absorbed in the details of their relocation, they accepted Tess's offer to spare their small son hours of boredom by keeping him busy at the Inn.

Within days of Matthew's arrival, she and Claire were on hands and knees admiring the small cities he constructed, enthusiastically taping his artwork on the kitchen cabinets, and struggling to recall the lyrics of childhood songs. One morning after Tess had left him with crayons and paper in the sitting room, she found it vacant when she brought in a snack and discovered him, at last, in the ballroom with Evan. He was hammering short nails into a wood scrap with a hammer proportioned to his size.

Evan met her gaze with a smile.

"I see you have an apprentice," she observed as she knelt beside Matthew and set the tray down.

"Know what, Tess? Look what Evan brought me," Matthew tipped the hammer up and began unscrewing its base.

"They get littler and littler." His high-pitched voice was a squeal of enthusiasm as he removed progressively smaller screwdrivers and lined them up on the floor.

"Well, look at that!" Tess leaned forward to survey the assortment, the smallest, barely an inch long. "Who'd have thought you could fit all those in there?"

"I use them for this," Matthew told her around the cookie he had stuffed into his cheek, and moved the board closer so she could see that it was studded with tiny bolts. "See?" A cloud of crumbs showered the floor. "Evan put them in, so I can take them out." He snatched up one of the screwdrivers in a starfish-shaped hand and loosened a bolt after several over-zealous tries.

"Take bites, now," Tess admonished gently.

"These are just precious," she smiled at Evan.

"I was about his age when I first used them," Evan said as he pulled himself to his feet. He leaned over Matthew's dark head and helped loosen a bolt that had been screwed in too tightly for small hands.

"These look awfully good, Matthew." He helped himself to a cookie from the plateful Tess had brought.

"Save your appetite." She glanced at her watch. "I've got a chicken roasting."

"You keep tempting me with these menus, I'll be dragging this job out longer than I need to." He fell into step beside her as she moved toward the door. "I should get the first coat of polyurethane on today and have this finished in two days."

"Oh, good," she said. "That'll leave us a few days' grace before the dance."

"All done," Matthew chirruped as he wiped a mustache of milk on his sleeve and eyed them curiously. "How come you walk like that, Evan?"

Evan's brows shot up as his mouth worked uncertainly.

The question hung in the air as expectantly as the look on the young questioner's guileless face. Something froze in Tess as she looked away from Evan's.

He turned and walked toward the boy, pausing to tousle his hair. "Well, you see, I wasn't careful enough one time, and I hurt my leg."

"How did you hurt it?" Matthew's eyes were like brown liquid as they looked up.

"I—I had a fall, and it got broken."

"Couldn't they fix it?"

"Oh, yes, they did the best they could."

"But it still makes you walk funny?"

Evan smiled as he nodded. "Yes, it does. I guess maybe that's its way of helping me remember to be more careful."

Matthew nodded, seeming satisfied with this answer.

Tess slowly released the breath she'd been holding and turned toward the door.

"Tell me," Evan called after her. "Have you a partner for the dance Friday night?"

Tess turned slowly, unwilling to believe what he might be proposing. Claire had been forthright in saying Evan wouldn't be likely to dance, just as Tess had wondered about the possibility. Claire demonstrated a growing knack for reading her thoughts.

"I don't know. Things may get busy. I've never done that sort of dancing ..."

"Well, if my only competition is a list of excuses, I'd like to offer myself. Surely if someone who walks funny can handle it, a little inexperience won't get in your way." He wiggled his brows ludicrously at Matthew, who erupted with giggles.

Tess's laughter chimed in. "I'd be delighted to test your theory. Thank you."

•

"It occurs to me that I owe you a meal or two," Evan said from where he stood at the kitchen door a few days later. The last coat of polyurethane was on the ballroom floor and he was packing up supplies.

"That's the understatement of the century," Claire said from where she was stirring a pot of sauce at the stove.

He grinned. "Any chance you two are free this evening?"

"Who's cooking?" Claire wondered.

"The host, of course."

"Afraid I'm booked but perhaps this girl's brave enough." Claire gave a small cough and gestured toward where Tess was reviewing bills at the table.

"Claire!" She raised her head abruptly. "That's not very nice!"

"Who says you have to be nice to be truthful?"

"You don't know what you're missing." Tess smiled warmly at Evan. "I'd love to come. What time are you serving?"

He shrugged. "Any time that fits your schedule. Shall we say around seven?"

"Perfect. Can I bring anything?"

"Only your appetite. Sure you won't change your mind, Claire?"

"Too close to my bedtime, thank you all the same. You two have a good time." Her features softened as she glanced up at him.

The Inn's dinner crowd consisted only of Matthew's family and two other couples that night and Claire dismissed Tess from the kitchen firmly just after 6:30.

She hurried upstairs to change into jeans and a sweater.

The drive seemed to take forever as she retraced the route in the dark. Although the temperature had dropped again, the air was still unusually warm for February. A thaw had already melted most of the snow and made her eager for spring, although Claire had warned her there would be numerous false alarms before then.

She rolled the window down a crack and inhaled the smell of the sea's ozone as she hurried along Snow Fence Road. The light from Helmut's old headlamps jounced crazily as they picked their way along the dirt track and alighted on the dark hulk of Evan's house.

The front door opened quickly at her knock. Evan took her coat and bolted back to the stove to remove a sheet of garlic bread from the oven in the nick of time, sucking his finger loudly when the small potholder proved insufficient insulation between the pan and his damp hands. "Claire's sauce smelled so good, I thought we might have pasta. Not very haute cuisine, I'm afraid."

"Who needs haute cuisine? Want any help?"

He shook his head and guided her somewhat awkwardly toward the table where he had set two places with the china that matched her eyes. Flickering light from a chunky candle in the center of the table cast huge shadows on the wall.

"Is it too dark?" he wondered anxiously, moving toward the kitchen light switch.

"Not if you can see what you're doing." She sat in the chair he pulled out for her and watched his thoughtful face as he drained the linguine. "Can I serve the salad?" she offered, reaching toward a big wooden bowl of greens crowned with tomato and mushroom slices.

"Please do," he replied from where he stood at the stove. He turned the heat down low under the sauce and brought the plates he'd heaped with pasta over to the table.

"Bet I know who made these," Tess said as she filled the small wooden bowl at his place from the larger one.

"Hmm?" He glanced up from where he was tossing the linguine on his plate in the sauce he'd ladled on top. "Oh, my father made those, actually."

"Is he the one who taught you to cook?"

"Well, he tried," Evan smiled, "but it was mostly necessity that did that."

"Necessity did a good job," Tess said as she tasted the sauce.

He thanked her and handed her the plate of garlic bread.

"Drinks!" He clapped his forehead and reached for their empty glasses as he rose. "Let's see, I've got orange juice, spring water, milk." He gave the wax container a loud sniff. "No, scratch that. Uh gee, I guess that's about it."

"Water's fine, thanks." Tess twisted a slice of bread into irregular halves.

"Probably should've got some wine," he said apologetically as he set the glass at her place and reclaimed his chair.

"I almost brought a bottle along but Claire said you didn't drink."

"No, I pretty much gave that up." He shrugged sheepishly. "Put away enough for a lifetime once, for ... ah ... medicinal purposes."

"Would have been the wrong color, anyhow," Tess said as she twirled her fork in the long, flat pasta.

The stereo provided a background of Mozart as they chatted over the meal. He intercepted her as she moved to fill the sink after he'd stacked the dishes in it. Placing his hands lightly on her shoulders, he turned her in the direction of the living room.

"I thought I might make a little after-dinner music, or at least I call it music," he said. "That is, if you don't mind."

The confusion on her face disappeared when she spied the instrument as she wandered toward the couch. She suppressed a small gasp of surprise.

The applewood trapezoid was about a yard across, resting on a wooden stand in the corner of the room. A chill roamed her spine as she crept toward the dulcimer and ran her fingers gently across the numerous pairs of strings that spanned the soundboard. The sound holes were fashioned like pinwheels, one on each side of the flat surface.

This was a much finer piece than the rustic version Andy had played. A lump rose in her throat at the thought of what it would be like to hear this again.

"Like to try it?" Evan reached past her and retrieved the slender hammers, pressing them into her hand before he moved to turn off the stereo.

She looked at them helplessly and remembered the well-worn one whose handle had finally snapped off as Andy had played for her one day. The broken tip was now stored on her bureau in Evan's minute replica of the Spinnaker, together with the handful of photographs she never looked at anymore.

She shook her head as she handed the hammers back. "I'll leave that to you."

A chill penetrated her limbs as she inched back toward the couch. She steeled herself against the rising memories, determined not to let them spoil the evening.

Tinny sounds rang out as Evan let the hammers fall onto the strings.

"Why didn't I notice this when I poked around here?" She pushed the words out past a growing tightness in her throat.

"It spent the last few winters with a friend of mine down south." He drummed out a random snatch of tune to warm up. "This isn't the one I'm proudest of, but I'm glad to have it back."

He launched slowly into a piece that he identified as *O'Carolan's Concerto*. Tess watched the concentration in his features as the sounds echoed off the cathedral ceiling. His upper body swayed as he lost himself in making music. This was obviously a much more developed ability for Evan than the experimenting Andy had done.

Flashes of moments almost forgotten came flowing back as she listened, unexpected memories of the good times with Andy before the surgeries. Before the cancer's growth had gotten too relentless to allow for any real hope.

Tess relaxed back against the couch, letting remembered happiness replace the initial stab of uncertain pain this had roused. When the music died away, she urged him to continue. He obliged with a few more songs before he set the hammers down and drew a bright serape blanket over the dulcimer.

"Thank you," Tess said quietly.

"My pleasure. I don't generally have an audience." He bent over the woodstove and started a fresh log in the fire. "Would you like some tea?"

She nodded, watching as he moved to the kitchen to put the kettle on.

When he returned, he lowered his tall frame onto the couch and reached to massage his knee. He had seated himself a carefully spaced distance from her that left just enough room for someone else to sit comfortably between them. She almost giggled when she thought of asking who he expected to join them. But perhaps he, too, was aware of the ghostly memories that lingered at the edges tonight.

His hair shone tawny in the faint light. Her eyes wandered involuntarily to where his flannel shirt was open at the throat, imagining the smoothness of the skin above his collarbone. There had been a time when nothing, no one would have eclipsed thoughts of Andy, but Evan's presence, palpable around her, was doing that very nicely indeed.

When he stretched an arm along the back of the couch, his fingertips brushed the patterned sleeve of the pullover she wore. "This is ... pretty. Very soft."

She smiled uncertainly. "My mother knitted it. For Christmas."

"Will she be coming up again soon?"

"In about a month. Would you like to meet her?"

After a pause, he said, "Uh ... sure. Yes, I would."

"I know she'd like to meet you."

"She would?" His eyes showed surprise.

Tess hesitated, unsure how to answer. "Yes, she's ... known about you. Much longer than I have, actually."

"Oh," he looked away quickly.

"What I mean is—" Tess was anxious she'd strayed too far again. "She knew about you somehow. My mother has a sort of understanding. She knows what's true even when things may appear different on the surface. Do you know what I mean?"

"I'm not sure." He shrugged.

"She knows things. She can tell when something's going to happen, or already has, but before anybody else ..."

"She's psychic?" Evan asked matter-of-factly.

"Well, sort of. Sometimes."

"Did she know what was going to happen to me?" he asked quietly.

"No, but ... once it had, she ... knew that things weren't what they seemed—what some people thought ..." She trailed off, uncertain how to continue.

"It's all right, Tess." The fingers that rested near her arm brushed her shoulder reassuringly.

"She was staying here in Knowle that summer at the Spinnaker. After you—after it happened—" Tess shifted, groping for words as he said nothing.

"She was very concerned for you. She told me about it. I just didn't piece it all together or remember until recently. It confused me then, but I understand a little better now." She shook her head. "This must all just sound strange …"

"No, it doesn't." His eyes were almost turquoise in the dim light. "It makes more sense to me than you might think.

"You know—" He rubbed his mouth with the back of his hand. "My dad never stopped talking about my mother—as though she were still alive, just somewhere else. Whenever something big was going on for me, I'd have dreams of her—her face. When I got hurt, her face was right there. It was more a feeling than something I actually saw. Kind of like an embrace of … safety or something. What you're telling me's not something I find hard to believe. It just surprises me."

"My mother was very happy when you came up in conversation at Christmas," Tess told him. "She'd had a dream about you, just a short time ago."

"What did she dream?"

"Unfortunately, she didn't say."

His eyes gleamed brightly. "Maybe she knows something we don't."

"Perhaps so, I don't know. I don't think I necessarily want to know the future anyway, even if it's possible."

"Me, either." He shook his head. "What would life be without anticipation?"

From the periphery of her vision, Tess saw he was watching her as he raked one hand through his hair absently. Then very slowly, he narrowed the space between them until he could trace a finger lightly along her brow bone and coax a stray lock of her hair behind her ear.

"I'm not very adept at this … part of the conversation." His expression seemed apologetic as she turned toward him. He withdrew his hand along the back of the couch and braced his chin in his palm, half-hiding his face.

"What do you want to say?"

"I'm not sure I can put it into words."

"How else can you tell me?" She laid her hand on his arm.

Closing his hand around it, he turned it upward to place a soft kiss in her palm. "I'm so glad you're here. In Knowle, I mean."

"I am, too."

"I ... don't exactly know where to go from here," he said.

"Where do you want to go?" Her face was inches from his now.

He cupped her chin and traced the edges of her mouth delicately. His breath felt warm as his lips moved near hers. "I'm afraid I'll say too much."

"Impossible. I'm a great listener." She pressed the kiss into fact, just as the kettle gathered steam to alert them with a piercing shriek that the water was ready.

"Damn!" He leapt to his feet to silence it.

Tess rose slowly and wandered about the room.

"I've got ice cream here," he called from the kitchen. "Shall we have it now?"

"Sure." She moved toward the refrigerator.

He looked surprised when he turned toward it to find her already removing two quart-sized containers from the freezer.

"Chocolate Mocha Chip and Rocky Road! You are good to me. How will I ever choose?"

"You'll have to have some of each." His eyes met hers as he took the containers from her and set them on the counter. "Talk about lousy timing, huh?"

"You were saying?" she wondered.

He drew her against him and rocked her back and forth, rubbing his chin across the crown of her hair. "I don't know what I'm saying. All I can think about is how empty it will feel here after you go."

"Guess you'll have to ask me back."

He turned toward the counter and spooned up a mouthful of the cocoa-colored ice cream and offered her a taste, watching her face as she savored it. "I may have just discovered the best way to lure you here."

She took the spoon and helped herself to more. "You may, at that."

She regarded him thoughtfully then reached to lace her fingers into his hand. "I think there's no rush, Evan. For anything. We're getting to know each other, and we can take our time."

He nodded as he gave her hand a squeeze. "I may have to ask you to help me remember that."

Chapter 8

The day of the dance dawned clear but cold. Wind shook the window sashes as Claire sneezed endlessly into an over-sized handkerchief. Her nose was a bright beacon of the miserable battle she was losing to a raging cold as she reached for her coat.

"Let me go to Rowan's," Tess insisted. "I'd like to get out, and you should be lying down somewhere."

"Can't lie down unless I'm going to sleep, and I never do that until it's dark." Claire sighed before a wrenching cough shook her.

"You really do sound awful. Just hold the fort for a little while, then you can take the afternoon off."

"I won't remind you about the dance tonight. I really must be sick. I'm too worn out to argue with you."

"Put some lemon juice in that, and a big spoonful of honey." Tess indicated the mug of hot water in which Claire was swirling a well-used teabag.

"Yes, doctor."

"I won't be long," Tess promised over her shoulder as she stepped outside. The bitter cold made her hurry, and she reached the harbor quickly.

The blast of heat that hit her in Rowan's kitchen felt like opening an oven door. The air was rich with the smell of chicken broth. A lone can with a red-and-white label sat on the carving board beside the stove and the soup's simmering rattled the lid on the pot as it spewed a ring of amber spots around the burner. The kettle moaned on the low heat that prevented its full boil.

Tess poked her head into the studio where Rowan squinted before a large canvas. "Shall I serve lunch, then?"

"Oh, Tess! I was hoping Claire would have the sense to stay

inside today. Sorry to trouble you, though. I meant to call to say I'd fix lunch myself but I seem to have lost track of the time. Make yourself something and join me, won't you?

"I see you've already had a little buffet." Her gaze swept beside him to the littered tabletop whose surface was strewn with paper wrappers full of cold cuts. The house's hot dry air had already curled the edges of the Swiss cheese.

"I invalidate the efforts of the most competent housekeepers." He shook his head.

"Never mind—you've more pressing business." She carried the packets to the refrigerator, put them away, then served the soup and poured the tea. Rowan cleared space on the table as she arrived with the tray. Then he crumbled crackers into his bowl.

Tess studied the painting on his easel, a view of the harbor that was all icy blues and grays. The pilings of distant piers across the charcoal-colored water were encased in hunks of dark ice and the late-day light etched the indigo sky with vivid magenta.

She remembered the painting above Evan's bed.

"I'm just puttering," Rowan said. "I felt like I'd die if I didn't get this down. Now my memory has betrayed the model, who's been too fickle to show her colors again."

An image took shape in Tess's head, the nearly iridescent shades of that other winter sunset with colors much warmer than these. "I saw this wonderful painting. It was a sunset, too, a view from the ballroom at the Inn. The detail was so exact."

"Where?" Rowan turned fully to face her.

"At Evan's house."

"Evan's?" His voice was incredulous.

She nodded. "I forgot to ask him about it. The visit was rather confusing." Her hand explored the side of her scalp as she remembered.

Rowan was staring straight past her. "It can't be."

"Whose is it?" she asked. "I looked for a signature but there was only some sort of little character."

"Were there other paintings like it?" The brush he clasped in his fist was quivering.

"The only others I saw were both landscapes of yours." She extended his tea mug toward him. He set the brush down and took it. "Do you know this painting?"

His face was pale as his navy-blue eyes met hers. "I'm not sure. Please. Go upstairs ... the front bedroom." He seemed to have difficulty forming the words.

"Rowan, what's wrong?" Tess was on her feet.

"Have a look at the paintings there."

She moved to make her way up the stairs, glancing back at him several times.

He sat frozen like a statue and didn't meet her eyes.

When she reached the front bedroom, her gaze wandered automatically to the portrait of Evan. There were changes in this room since the last time she'd seen it. Paintings were set five- or six-deep against two of its walls. Tess could see immediately that the artist must be the same as the one whose work she'd just described.

There were a variety of canvases here: a still life whose glossy vases held a reflected world in precise miniature, a pencil drawing of a silken scarf draped as though someone had just dropped it to the intricately patterned carpet on which it rested. Tess could almost feel the cool smoothness of its folds.

She flipped through the canvasses with reverent care. Landscapes, more still lifes, scenes of bustling activity, crowded with human forms. Most had the same small oriental character etched in thin black lines in a corner of the canvas. Tess knelt before them. Each had that quality of light as clear as the flawless application of color on its surface.

She noticed the portrait of Evan again and searched the canvas until she found the tiny character half hidden in a fold of his shirt near the base. A "young protégé" was how Rowan had described this artist, Tess remembered now. But who?

She had her answer when she investigated one last stack of paintings against the adjoining wall. Beneath a view of a brilliant summer garden and two small still lifes was a three-quarter-length portrait whose face was instantly familiar. Tess slid it out of the stack and set it in front of the others.

It was a self-portrait, of course, a beautiful heart-shaped face crowned with billows of reddish-gold hair. The subject's head was tipped back, the green eyes unfocused, contemplative, like orbs of clear glass. A cleft marked the fine promontory of the upturned chin. The hands resting in the lap were like small birds, fingers curled skyward, a single, slender brush cupped in one of the upturned palms.

"Celia." Tess breathed the name aloud.

The face was ethereal, wafting on the canvas as if composed of vapors, for all the photographically precise lines of draftsmanship that had captured it.

Tess saw the same sadness in the eyes as she had in the newspaper photograph. All this powerfully creative beauty from such delicate hands—a face so beautiful and so vulnerable.

Rowan was spooning soup slowly and raised his face when she came downstairs.

"They're absolutely breathtaking," she told him quietly.

"Then they are the same?"

"Yes. They're Celia's, aren't they?"

Rowan nodded.

"How long have you had them?"

"They were in the Spinnaker's attic. Claire saw to it they were safe."

"Does Evan know about them?"

Rowan nodded. "He's seen them all, at one time or another, but probably thought her family had them, just as I did."

"Do they have others?"

"Most likely, if time and neglect haven't warped or destroyed them." His mouth was a tight, angry line. "They had absolutely no understanding of what ability she had. Tried to hound her into the things they thought were important, and painting would never be one of those."

He pounded his leg with his fist. "They worked against everything in her that was important. Defeated her at every turn. She spent her life trying to please them but they never cared about anything that really mattered to her."

His face was ashen, his body rigid with impotent anger as Tess watched with growing alarm. "What do you plan to do with the paintings?"

"Someone I know started a gallery in Portland about a year ago. She's been after me to exhibit there, but this must come first."

"She's going to show Celia's work?"

"If all goes as planned. The exhibit is scheduled to open about two weeks from now." Rowan affirmed. "I'll need help, of course."

There was urgency in his tone as he gestured toward his stooped frame. "I'll pay someone to get them there—"

"No," Tess broke in. "Let me do it."

"Oh, I can't ask you to do that."

"I want to do it. I can see how special they are." The evanescent image of Celia's face floated before her. "They should be where lots of people can see them."

Rowan couldn't disguise his pleasure, even as he warned her, "This isn't going to be an easy matter, Tess."

"How hard can it be? You've already made the arrangements. All you'll need is someone to get them there safely. It's simply a matter of borrowing something big enough to transport them. Maybe Evan can—"

"I'm not planning to involve him in this, Tess," Rowan said emphatically.

She turned to him, surprised. "Why not?"

"Claire seems to feel he's not ready for it, and she's already skittish enough about bringing them out. That's why I've arranged to get the exhibit up while he's away."

"Away?" Tess felt a flutter of apprehension. "Where?"

"He's going up north for a week or so, at the end of the month."

Tess took this in. "Well, surely he's going to hear about it sooner or later?"

Rowan dabbed at his mouth with a handkerchief. "If my instincts are correct, these will go much farther than Portland. My hope is that by the time he does find out, their reception will make him more amenable to the idea."

His expression seemed to plead for understanding. "It's better this way, Tess. Easier on him, certainly. If only Claire had come forward with these sooner we could have had them in New York by now." He sighed. "I suppose it has helped put more distance between Evan and—the accident. But we can't lose any more time. My name can help speed things along, but not from the grave."

The resignation in his voice touched Tess as deeply as the beauty of Celia's unknown work. How hopeless he must have felt about it all these years. She knew that lonely feeling all too well. "This is very important to you, isn't it?"

"More than you know. I came here too late to be any real help to her and this may be my last chance." He raised his eyes to meet hers. "Your confidence about this—"

" ... is assured," she broke in. "If you really think it's best. You've known him much longer than I have."

His smile was pleased. "Thank you, Tess. Thank you for understanding."

"Her work deserves to be seen. But why did she sign it that way?"

"It means 'no one,'" Rowan said. "Like any artist, she couldn't stop painting, even with all the discouragement, but could never seem to own the talent she had."

"Her eyes look so sad," Tess said.

"There were too many compromises in her life for any real happiness."

"Well, now her work can bring others pleasure."

Tess grew more anchored in the rightness of this as she hurried back to the Inn under a leaden sky that boded snow. When doubts about Evan intruded on her excitement, she reasoned that Celia's work surely meant a great deal to him. He might even be grateful if others did this on her behalf.

After Andy's death, she'd felt confounded by the things she couldn't do, couldn't change. But here was a way she could actually help.

•

Claire insisted that she felt well enough to help out with the contra dance after Tess had enforced an afternoon of complete rest.

Evan arrived at the Inn just after sunset and joined in to help with the mealtime rush, which was busier than usual. When the band arrived to set up, Tess led the way to the ballroom, where Evan had spread a thin layer of sawdust so the newly varnished floor wouldn't prove too slippery underfoot.

By 7:30, the dancers were arriving in bunches. Soon the room was so well populated Tess made a silent prayer that the floorboards would hold up.

The sounds of fiddle and piano filled the air and lured even the most obstinate observers out onto the floor. The caller, a small woman in a swirling patchwork skirt, seemed pleased with the determination of her participants as she taught the sets. When Tess carried in trays of cider and cheese, she had to press against the wall to accommodate the crowd of dancers who seemed to be running out of room.

Matthew's father had claimed Claire, despite her protests. Matthew looked very grown up as he wove through the set with his mother. By tomorrow night, they'd be settled in their new home. She'd miss Matthew's company, and his impending departure made her all the more aware that Evan's work here was finished, too.

As the set drew to a close, Tess joined the spirited applause. Then she felt a hand close around her wrist.

"Time to bite the bullet," Evan's voice pressed near her ear.

Drawing a breath, she laid her hand lightly on the arm he extended toward her and followed him out as the caller began a new set.

She frowned in concentration, trying to commit the caller's instructions to memory and joined Evan's laughter when they both flubbed inevitably. As the dance progressed, his face was replaced by a series of others, old and young, and by the time he reappeared before her, she was feeling moderately proficient and let her shoulders relax.

"You're an old hand at this, aren't you?"

"But it's been years," he protested and whirled her into a dizzying swing that was surely more than the caller had asked for. His endurance seemed to grow as he kept her out on the floor for dance after dance. His eyes glittered with pleasure each time their hands joined. Just once he released her to begin the dance with a different partner, and only because it was Matthew who asked.

She ducked into the kitchen for more refreshments during the band's break and Evan reclaimed her the instant the music began again. They became hopelessly lost in a more complex contra dance. She was huffing along behind him as he struggled to keep up with their disappearing companions and she finally dissolved against him in mirth as the set broke up in roar of defeated laughter.

"Alas, I have disgraced you." He laid an arm across his eyes as he led her to the edge of the room and leaned against the wall, face damp from his exertion.

"I never knew disgrace could be so much fun!"

"Anything with you can be fun." His voice was husky and his words brought a shiver as the cold cider he'd poured for her slid past her throat.

His eyes swept the length of the plum-colored dress she wore. "And everything's more beautiful."

"I think you're too exhausted to see straight," she teased.

"Me? Never!" He took her glass and set it down on the ledge beside them.

She followed him eagerly as he led her by the hand and the band began a waltz.

"No interruptions this time," he murmured in her ear.

She was breathless, with nowhere to look but into those aquamarine eyes. He guided her with quick grace, his uneven gait disappearing as he glided her about.

Unexpected sounds from the refreshment table drifted above the music.

Tess turned to see Claire dodging the dancers around them, her face a mask of fear as she gestured frantically for their attention.

It was Evan who first realized the cause of Claire's alarm and broke off to race toward the small figure surrounded by a growing crowd of panicked dancers. Tess was just beginning to take in what had happened when the musicians trailed off uncertainly. Then someone screamed and a dozen voices began talking at once.

Evan thrust his way through the knot of frenzied bodies and pulled Matthew free. One starfish hand clutched at his throat. With a sliding sound, followed by a crash of glass, the tablecloth pulled free in the grip of the other small hand that clasped its folds.

Time stood still for Tess. In hasty flashes, she saw the child's hand, which became an older one in which not a tablecloth, but a stark white sheet was balled.

Bile rose instantly in her throat as she watched Evan through a stinging blur. In a sense of motion sickeningly slowed into terrifying frames, she saw him set the small body before him and reach around to clasp his fists against the pudgy abdomen.

A roar filled her ears as her fingers clawed the wall against which she'd lurched, unsure how she'd gotten there from the middle of the dance floor, fighting with every ounce of strength to keep from slipping to the floor as the room turned to gray fuzz and swam around her. Every instinct in her body pushed her back from the room's focal point even as her mind screamed that she should move toward it.

After Evan made a few gentle thrusts, Matthew sputtered, then burst into incensed sobs as the obstruction in his windpipe popped free.

The pressure in Tess's chest was a rising volcano as she backed away, jarred by quick glimpses of the rush of relief that filled the room. Evan hugging Matthew against him, apologizing for the fear his desperate action had caused. Matthew's mother tearfully expressing gratitude as his father took the child from Evan's arms and a cacophony of sound filled the room.

Tess groped her way into the dim light of the hall and barely reached the small bathroom before collapsing over the sink with violent retching. Her body heaved in empty effort until a rain of wrenching tears burst forth.

Every inch of her seemed to be turning to liquid. She shivered with the icy cold of the clamminess that drenched her, washed her legs out from under her. The hands she pressed over her face couldn't contain the torrent that pried loose from months of tight control—it poured back with startling intensity, these memories she'd worked so hard not to think about, what she'd swallowed inside.

A fairytale snowfall had begun early that gray day in western Massachusetts, with impossibly fluffy flakes that mounted up quickly. In her twelfth hour of work, Tess had heard the calls come in one after another, half the evening staff of her medical-surgical floor had a commute from outlying towns and wouldn't make it in. Andy had tried to distract her from her exhausted anxiety, his face pallid as she'd fussed about his hospital bed, wishing they could both be free of this place that drained them—Andy, because of the endless chemotherapy and surgeries that weren't going to stop the ravage of his cancer, and Tess, who'd given out too much for too long.

She had never faced the inevitability of his death. She'd been too focused on getting him away to where she'd be able to care for him—try other means she believed would be a remedy but which, she knew now, would have come too late to save him.

He had been so vital, so worthy of life, and she had been so clever in denying his impending death, evading her anger about it, grasping at straws of hope in her rage that this should be his fate.

On that wretched night, so vivid in memory now, she had left him reluctantly to tend to the multitude of tasks that came with the dinner hour on a busy hospital floor. In the ten short minutes before she returned to check on his progress, Andy Hollinger, the only man whose life she ever considered merging with her own, had choked to death as he sampled solid food for the first time in several days. There had never been any question of accountability as she had turned all her anger and rage upon herself.

Huddled over the sink now, she felt like the only person in the universe, so lonely with this pain that pounded in her brain, miles from everyone and everything as anger and helplessness and, finally, the wound of unbearable loss shook her.

Hours seemed to have passed when she reached to run cold water over her wrists and bathe her aching face. At some point, someone knocked on the door as she pressed against it while the two taps gushed water, her self-protective effort to mask the sound of the keening that had come from deep inside her, such ancient grief. The footsteps had finally moved away but Tess had remained frozen against the door.

Every inch of her felt wrung out as she made useless attempts to hide the devastation that had wracked her swollen features. Finally, she cracked the door and leaned against it, still unwilling to leave her self-imposed prison. Only a handful of voices echoed in the ballroom, the sounds of the musicians packing up their instruments, and the lingering guests who still discussed, with relieved disbelief, the awful turn of events that had completely inverted Tess's world.

•

Evan's cheeks puffed out in an exhausted exhalation as he helped carry the last few items from the ballroom into the kitchen.

Claire took his hand and squeezed it in both of hers as the door from the dining room swung shut behind him. "Lord help us, that was too close. I owe you my life as much as the boy does, for being so quick."

"We all have a little stake in his future," Evan sighed in weak relief. "What happened to Tess?"

As he spoke, Claire drew a sharp breath, gazing past him to where Tess was weaving in unsteady silence toward the stove.

Evan's eyes widened at he looked at her.

She knew her face looked ravaged, with deep shadows under her eyes. She fought to stand erect.

Evan stepped toward her and brushed her cheek with his fingers. "Hey—it's all right, Tess." He tipped her chin up gently, smile encouraging. "He's fine, now."

She stepped back and dropped her gaze, still shaking as she hugged herself tightly, trying to make it stop.

"Dear girl, what is wrong?" Claire asked in alarm.

"It's … nothing. I'll be fine." The words eked out between teeth she clenched to keep them from chattering.

Evan put an arm around her shoulders and exchanged a look with Claire. "You can manage?"

"Of course." Claire crossed the room, took Tess's other arm, and turned her in the direction of the hall. Her head gestured past Evan toward the sitting room off the foyer.

Evan led Tess into it and shut the door behind them. A small lamp gave off low, comforting light and a fire had dwindled to glowing embers in the hearth.

He drew her toward a loveseat and guided her down onto it by the shoulders then took the heavy afghan that lay across the back and tucked it around her.

She shook her head helplessly. "I should have been there. I just froze." She added with disgust, "I did nothing."

"I was there first," Evan countered. "You didn't have a chance."

"I couldn't move." She covered her face. "Couldn't stop seeing…"

"What?" He sat beside her and pulled her hands away. "What did you see?"

Then he drew her against the nubby wool of his sweater as a sob wrenched from inside her, smoothed her hair as she gave up against him like a child.

"Talk to me," he said gently. "You've waited a long time. Did you think I hadn't noticed? Don't you know it's like looking in a mirror for me? What did you see?"

"Someone—who didn't have any help. Until it was too late." Her voice gave way.

"In the hospital?"

She nodded violently.

Then she told him. About the hands that had pulled her off the bed as she fought to continue her hopeless task. How righteous she'd always been about the immorality of trying to resuscitate someone with a terminal illness. She'd spent every ounce of her strength trying to revive him. Grasp back a life she couldn't imagine living without.

She'd heard the whispered speculation: that her refusal to accept the inevitable was just the exhaustion of her double shift, the shock of being the first to find him.

Anger rose now as Tess remembered the most thoughtless words: *It's probably better this way.* She'd have struck whoever said them, but too many hands had held her before she'd collapsed. Endless help had been there once Andy was beyond helping.

"Don't you know yourself well enough to believe you did everything you could?" Evan's voice was low near her ear.

"He was doing so well—going home soon." Her hand balled into a fist she pressed to her mouth as she shook her head, unbelieving. "I thought he was safe because he was feeling so much better." Her voice faltered. "Because … I was there. But then I left him alone." Her voice was weighted with condemnation. "And I never heard him."

She described how Mrs. Flaherty's arthritic moaning had drowned out everything as Tess tried to coax her to eat unpalatable food. The only other nurse had been at the other end of the corridor cleaning up the tray a man had hurled to the floor.

Another tray had crashed to the floor, as the endless buzzers demanded help where there was no one free to give it.

Tess described the scene she'd discovered: Andy's tortured face, blue rapidly growing gray, the tray of multi-colored fluids in a grotesque mixture of glass shards at the foot of the bed, his hand clenched around the rail. Where the string for the call light should have been. The one she forgot to put back in her fussy efforts to make him comfortable. Joking about the meals she'd cook to redeem the assault of hospital food she'd urged on him all those weeks.

At last, she fell silent.

Evan rocked her back and forth against him. "Did you love him very much?"

She nodded, gasping in her effort to regain breath. "He was twenty-nine, and had so little time left. I wanted to do everything I could to make it good for him."

"And you did." The look in Evan's eyes was insistent.

"I really would like to believe that."

"Did you think keeping this buried was going to help you believe it?"

"I had to … put it away. So I could bear to keep going."

He shook his head. "That's like trying to bury a beach ball in the water. It doesn't matter how hard you press down, it always pops up somewhere else."

She hiccupped and made a small frown at the homespun truth of his imagery. "Well, what about you?"

"What about me?"

Tess was unsure how to choose her next words.

His features were calm. "There's a difference between choosing not to—discuss something, and trying to deny it altogether."

His eyes probed hers. "I just don't happen to need to talk things out all that often. I've had a lot of time to work through them on my own."

"Have you?" she challenged.

"Enough to see pretty clearly when someone is walking around wounded because they haven't." His gaze was steady as he looked at her.

"I've soaked that sweater." She reached for tissues on the table next to the sofa.

"It's seen salt water before." He thumbed moisture from her cheeks and cupped them with his palms, then placed small kisses over her eyes, inching downward until he captured her mouth just briefly.

She curled into him when he tucked an arm around her shoulders and pulled her against his side. "Sweet Tess, you're too dear to stay trapped in your past."

Her tired eyes gleamed as they looked up at his. "I could tell you the same thing."

"Yes, I suppose you could." His mouth tugged in a smile. He pressed a kiss on her forehead before disengaging his arm to hoist himself laboriously to his feet. "This has been too long a day for everyone. Tonight we all need a good, sound sleep."

Then he remembered, "Rowan has a birthday in a few days."

"Yes, we thought we'd have a dinner for him here. Will you come?"

He nodded. "What time shall I bring him?"

"Around seven would be good." She stood slowly. "I don't know how to thank you for being here tonight."

"There's nothing you can thank me for that hasn't helped me just as much." Then he said, "I'm supposed to go up north at the end of the week. I'll be away ..."

"Rowan told me. Where are you going?"

"Some friends run a sawmill outside of Bangor. I go up there about this time every year when my own work is slow." The V-shaped furrow deepened between his brows. "I don't like the idea of leaving you. But I've already put this off twice."

"And it's important that you go. I'll be fine," she assured him. "How long will you be gone?"

"A week or so, at the most."

"You'll be missed," she said softly.

The aqua eyes twinkled. "I've never had a better reason to hurry back."

Chapter 9

Tess was stacking plates in the dining-room hutch when she heard them come in. For the special occasion, she'd twisted her long hair into a topknot, worn her favorite silver jewelry, and chosen a knitted dress the same blue-gray color as her eyes.

She heard Claire greet Evan by name in the foyer and her spine tingled at the timbre in his voice. She looked up to find him watching her from where he stood in the doorway. His dark sports coat made his shoulders seem especially broad.

In an instant, Rowan drew alongside him. "Look! It's another old man who's not dead yet!"

"Rowan! What a thing to say!" Tess stepped forward to take his hand and kiss his cheek. "You're an inspiration to us all."

She led them to the table she'd prepared near a window that looked out on the porch. In honor of the day, there would be no other diners. "Every table's reserved for you, Rowan."

Evan touched petals of the yellow roses in the center of the table. "I smelled these the minute we came in."

"No, my boy. That was a much fairer flower." Rowan caught Tess's hand and brought her wrist near his cheek. "That's what you often wear, isn't it? Attar of Rose?"

She nodded. "Would you all like a drink to start?"

Evan's face showed surprise. "Aren't you going to join us?"

"Only after I've cooked your meal."

"She insisted," Claire shrugged as Evan seated her next to Rowan. "We're in for a treat—we'll just have to do without her for a bit."

Rowan was methodically unfolding his napkin on his lap. "I'm afraid that my appetite's as old as the rest of me. Any wine to give it a prod?"

"Something pale, not too sweet?" Tess called from the butler's pantry off the dining room.

"That would be lovely."

"Anybody else?"

"Oh, why not?" Claire decided.

"Nothing for me, thanks," said Evan.

Tess returned with two stemmed glasses of Riesling then disappeared into the kitchen. She got their appetizers ready—slices of smoked salmon on tiny potato latkes with bits of onion, cooked egg, and a spoonful of capers—then served them.

When everyone had finished, she collected the plates and hurried back to the kitchen to drop fist-sized bunches of angel hair pasta into the water she'd brought to a boil. She had just enough time to steam asparagus before everything else was ready. They were having Rowan's favorite item from the Spinnaker's menu, a shrimp and scallop dish served in a cream sauce on top of the pasta.

Claire appeared exactly when needed to take the garnished plates out to the dining room. "I've had all I could do to keep birthday boy from stuffing himself on the bread." She smiled at the plates approvingly. "He'll certainly want to have room for this."

Rowan's exclamations of pleased surprise reached Tess's ears as she was taking the dessert out of the refrigerator. Then she hurried to join them.

They all assured her that she'd surpassed herself. This dish had been one of Dorothy Farragut's favorites and even Claire was apprehensive about tackling its recipe without overcooking everything. Evan remembered an attempt of his own the customer sent back, calling it more reminiscent of "Cream of Wheat Newburg."

"You always were coming up with new entrees of your own," Claire teased.

"Every cook improvises a little," he defended.

"Was that your word for it?" Her eyes sparked with humor as she intercepted Tess, who was reaching for their empty plates. "Your shift's over."

Tess reclaimed her seat without protest.

Claire reappeared a short while later with the small cheesecake

Tess had baked that morning, another of Rowan's favorites. Her eyes indicated the seven candles as she set the cake in front of him "I'm afraid fire codes only allow us to mark decades now."

After Claire poured coffee and they sang *Happy Birthday*, Rowan sat thoughtfully for a few moments before he blew out the candles.

"A good wish?" Evan asked as Tess cut them generous slices.

"Indeed," Rowan said as he looked at him. "One I'd love to see come true."

"Have you enjoyed the day?" Tess asked.

"It's been stellar. Evan helped me set up the easel outside."

"In the snow?" Claire was incredulous.

"Yes, in the snow," Rowan told her defiantly. "Bundled up so tight I could hardly hold my damn brush, don't worry."

Claire scowled at Evan, who shrugged helplessly.

"He said he wasn't going to paint another landscape indoors. You know how it is when he sets his mind to something."

"All too well," Claire fixed her gaze on Rowan. "Sometimes I think he's not only a fanatic, but a madman."

Rowan reached for her freckled hand and closed his gnarled one around it. "But I'm your favorite fanatic madman."

"Claire tells me you'll have a visitor tonight," Tess said.

Rowan nodded. "My daughter, Deborah. All in a tizzy about turning fifty. I convinced her to sit for me, promised to cast her as eternally youthful." After a pause, he said, "It's a shame none of them ever took an interest in painting."

"Perhaps they feel you've covered that territory enough for one family."

Tess sensed an unfamiliar edge in Claire's voice.

"Age makes one painfully aware of the absence of legacy, my dear."

Claire averted her eyes from Rowan's unblinking gaze and drained her coffee, then said dryly, "Only if one is an irascible old coot to begin with."

"Ah, the voice of my conscience." His face creased in a smile as he glanced from Tess to Evan.

"Didn't I hear that your son, Stephen, had a gallery?" Tess remembered.

Evan looked away quickly and Claire cut in before Rowan could reply. "He did, at one time. But that doesn't count."

The eyes she turned toward Evan's were very bright. "May I impose on you to help Tess manage here, while Rowan claims my company? I'd love to see Deborah."

"Of course," Evan smiled in assent. "I'd be delighted."

"This has been just lovely, Tess," Rowan said.

"I'm glad you've enjoyed it." She gave his cheek a resounding kiss, then gathered their empty dessert plates into a stack and moved to join Claire in the kitchen.

•

Evan helped Rowan to his feet and followed him to the foyer.

The older man studied Evan's face as he struggled into his overcoat. "Everything all right with you tonight? You seemed a bit more thoughtful than conversational."

"Just enjoying the company. Thinking it's probably about time I ... you know ..." He fingered his tie self-consciously as his head gestured toward the kitchen. "Sort of go for broke."

"Well! I don't believe it!" Rowan's face lit in an enormous smile. He lowered his voice as the sound of the women's laughter drew nearer. "After three-quarters of a century, my birthday wish may actually come true!"

•

The Inn was quiet after they waved Claire and Rowan off. Tess's heart fluttered as she moved about the kitchen while Evan cleared the last few things from the table. Each seemed to give their respective tasks inordinate attention.

The flutter increased when Tess heard his uneven gait halt just a few feet from her as his eyes surveyed her with their dancing light.

"I'll start dropping things if you keep looking at me that way."

He pocketed one hand and edged closer to where she stood at the sink. A finger brushed her flaming cheek and smoothed a lock of hair behind her ear. "I never paid my compliments to the chef properly." His voice was a low whisper as he reached to extract the handful of silverware she clasped and set it on the counter. "Better disarm you first." His tie swung forward awkwardly.

"Oh, God, Evan. You always do." She seized the striped silk in a playful tug.

He laughed softly then circled his arms around her waist from behind as he breathed in her scent. A long, slow sigh brushed past her ear.

"Tesssss." His lips pressed her hair, then her temple, before he settled his cheek against hers. "I'm completely in love with you. I don't know what I'm going to do."

She turned to face him. She felt heady at his nearness, awestruck at his words as she reached around his broad shoulders. "What's happening with us, Evan?"

"Only what's supposed to, I think."

His eyes gleamed as he lowered his mouth toward hers and she let herself be absorbed by the kiss.

Her hands explored his face—the furrow between his brows, the wide planes of his cheekbones, the strength of his jaw. When their lips connected again, she was supremely conscious of every point of contact throughout the length of them. A tingling glow rushed like a torrent from the crown of her head and when he pressed her against him with a low moan, she imagined he felt it, too.

He drew back at last and pulled impatiently at his tie, stuffing it into his jacket pocket. "You're all I think about." He shook his head. "I can't imagine how much I'll miss you when I go north."

"I can!" she said. Then added, "But it's not for that long, right? There've been plenty of longer stretches."

"Maybe, but I'm losing whatever tolerance I may have had for them."

Tess's gaze dropped away. "I have too much to say to know how to begin."

He laughed as his arms tightened around her. "Then I'll hope it takes you a lifetime to say it all."

She glanced toward the doorway of the sitting room off the hall. "Why don't you wait for me in there while I put these last few things away?"

"Let me help."

She shook her head and pushed him away. "I don't imagine you'd be a whole lot of help right now. And I need a chance to catch my breath!"

"Don't be long." His smiling mouth descended and took it away again. His physical nearness seemed almost dreamlike and unreal.

When she entered the sitting room a few minutes later, Evan had used the time to get flames crackling in the fireplace. He was studying Rowan's portrait of her, which Claire had recently hung over the mantel. The dimples alongside his mouth deepened as he caught hold of her hand and pulled her down onto his lap.

"I had it upstairs," Tess said self-consciously. "Claire insisted we put it up here."

"It belongs where we can see it," he said as his lips wandered along the nape of her neck. "I'd like it to be the first thing I see each day."

As she studied his face, she thought of Celia's portrait of him, and her paintings.

"Are you happy here, Tess?"

"Why, yes. I love it here."

"Happy enough to stay?"

She intercepted his hand as it reached involuntarily for his left knee, placing her own there and massaging gently. "Well, no other plans come to mind."

"You must think I'm crazy," he said. "I think I'm crazy—letting weeks go by without seeing you, scared to death. Figuring I'll let fate take its course. Terrified that if I actually do or say anything, I'll screw it all up."

"I love you, Evan," Tess told him. "I'm past worrying about what's crazy."

The light of the room's solitary lamp bathed his features in a warm glow as he tipped his head back to find her eyes. "After so much that didn't last, I guess I made myself hold back. I didn't want to be mistaken. Didn't know if I could face that."

She tightened her arms around his neck.

"I want to share life with you, Tess. Build my house big enough for you and whoever comes along to join us." He curled stray tendrils of her hair around his fingers. "Or help you here at the Spinnaker, if that's what you want."

"Or perhaps all of it. Somehow." She nestled against the slow, steady rhythm of his heart. "Nothing's been the same since I looked up to see you watching me help myself to your blueberries."

He kissed her with deliberate tenderness.

"I suppose I had a lot of the same fears." Tess said finally. "So, I decided that truly becoming your friend was the best place to start." She shook her head. "I've worked so hard to convince myself anything else is impossible, it feels like I'm going to wake up any minute now."

His chuckle was low. "In that case, we'll both wake up very disappointed."

As their lips came together again, he murmured, "My dearest, precious friend."

Chapter 10

Tess moved through her days in a haze in which time rolled away from her like a ball of yarn down a flight of stairs. Each night, she mentally reviewed what she'd been doing at that time on the evening she'd spent with Evan, before he'd headed north, lingering in memories of the look in his eyes or cadence of his voice.

The Spinnaker's phone rang one afternoon before the dinner rush. "For you," Claire called from the kitchen to where Tess was reading the Inn's guest register.

"Hello?" She held the receiver of the desk phone in place with her shoulder as she fumbled through the book's oversized pages.

"Good afternoon," Rowan's gravelly voice greeted her after the loud click of Claire's hanging up the extension.

"Oh, hi! I hear you had a nice visit the other night."

"Yes, indeed. Tell me, is there any chance you have some free time tomorrow?"

"I imagine so. What time?"

"Anytime you like between ten and five. I just spoke with Marielle, the gallery owner, and she'd like to have the paintings there tomorrow if it's possible."

The paintings! Tess hadn't given them much thought in the past week. "I should be able to do that. I'll just make sure Claire's all set."

"Tess, do me a favor—have you discussed this with her?"

"Uh, no. I haven't had a chance."

"I wonder if you'd hold off doing so, for a bit? You know how worried she gets, and I think this time she's wound up to really go on a rampage. If we just get them quietly to Portland and let her find out later how simple it was, without a lot of fuss, I really do think it would go easier on all of us."

"Well," Tess's voice held both uncertainty and surprise. Then she laughed. "Maybe she does have enough to think about. I don't seem to be much use around here this week."

"I'd appreciate it," Rowan said. "I talked with Dickie yesterday. How do you feel about using his van to take them in?"

Tess's thoughts flashed a quick image of what she'd look like driving the monstrous green van. "Well, it'll certainly be big enough!"

Rowan chuckled. "Then it's all set. I can't tell you what a relief it is to have your help with this."

"You really feel okay about this, Rowan?" She couldn't explain why, but an uncomfortable sensation of doubt was starting to rise inside her.

"Absolutely. The gallery and I both have insurance that will cover them."

"No, I mean, do you really feel comfortable with me doing this?" A stream of worst-case-scenarios was beginning to fill her mind as the weight of this responsibility occurred to her for the first time since she'd discussed it with him.

"Tess, I have waited so long." His voice sounded sad. "I couldn't feel better about this if I were able to drive them there myself."

His words seized her heart. "Are they all set to go?"

"They will be."

"I'll be there as soon as I can in the morning, probably about ten."

As she hung up, happy recollection of her evening with Evan quickly drew her away from the last of her doubts.

•

Dickie gripped the handle of the driver's door, which tilted imperfectly on its hinges as he held it open for Tess.

"She's gettin' old," he advised. "New brakes and shocks, though. Should handle just fine without rattlin' your baggage none."

"We really appreciate this, Dickie."

"Hell, it'd only be sittin' here. Glad to help y'out. Got a stick shift of your own, ain't ya?"

She nodded as she settled into the unaccustomed spaciousness of the seat and found the ignition. The van came to life on the first try, but shuddered into a stall after a few loud sputters like a dog shaking off fleas.

"Usually takes a few goes," Dickie said. "Should be plenty o' gas to get you there and back. No need to worry 'bout that. I got a pile o' blankets in back, if ya need 'em. Wrap stuff up in, I mean."

"Thanks." Tess studied the dashboard's unfamiliarity as the van idled steadily after a few false starts. "I'll just take it slow and easy."

"You bet. Have a good trip." He raised one massive hand as he backed away toward the store.

When Tess arrived at Rowan's house, she discovered that driving the van was like navigating a living room on wheels. She struggled to back it close to his front door.

The task was made even more challenging by the thick coating of ice that covered the gradual incline of his driveway, which saw little use. She finally had to admit defeat and face the prospect of staggering with the paintings over the vast expanse of slick surface between the house and the van.

Rowan had everything ready for her and apologized for the inconvenience of the ice. The paintings, covered securely in brown padded wrapping with hangers exposed for easy carrying, were arranged in orderly rows against the wall inside the door.

Tess carried each over the ice as carefully as if it were a baby. When they were all packed into the van, she ducked back inside out of the frigid wind blowing off the harbor.

"Here are the biographies, fresh from the printer." Rowan handed her a ream-sized cardboard box. "Marielle's expecting you. Tell her I'll call later this afternoon just in case she has any questions, all right?"

"I'll let you know when I get back." Tess hugged him and hurried outside.

In her enthusiasm to be off, she depressed the unfamiliar accelerator a little too hard. The van slid sideways, veering off a ridge at the edge of the drive that wasn't more than two inches high but left the rear wheels spinning helplessly with a frantic whine as she gunned the gas in panicked effort to free them.

With a sigh, she leapt from the driver's seat and discovered that Rowan had neither salt nor sand. At his suggestion, she checked the woodstove he used on the coldest nights and discovered a generous supply of ashes in the bottom. Clouds of gray dust swirled around her as she shoveled ashes into the pail Rowan brought.

Outside, she uttered a silent plea for help as she spread the ashes on either side of the van's rear wheels. After a seemingly infinite number of rockings back and forth, and further applications of the sooty substance, the van finally tore free and skidded down the drive to the dry surface of the harbor road.

Although the van's flat front gave Tess the advantage of an unobstructed view, she became aware how limited her depth perception was as she crept along the Village's main street. The alarm that registered in one man's face showed her just how narrowly she'd missed scraping the parked car on which his gaze was fixed.

She had wakened with an uneasy sense that was hard to define, but seemed to be growing more pronounced the farther she drove from Knowle. The drive to Portland would take about half an hour, but the unexpected developments had seen to it that she was already that much behind schedule.

She was riddled with guilt at the thought of Claire's having to manage alone for longer than planned, especially on a Friday when guests would be arriving.

There was rigid tension in her shoulders that seemed to be growing worse. A gnawing apprehension made her mid-section swim, and she had the peculiar feeling, impossible to explain, that somewhere not far away, fate was laughing—at her expense.

•

The green van on the overpass of the ramp onto the highway looked like Dickie's to Evan's tired eyes as he meandered off the exit that brought him closest to Knowle.

He had pushed himself hard ever since he'd first become aware that he was ahead of schedule when he left Pennsylvania the previous night. The roads had been clear and though the lumber truck he drove had only a receiver, the other truckers with whom he traveled not only kept him company but ensured he made excellent time within the confines of the law enforcement that arose like periodic landmarks on the road. When he'd paused with the other drivers at the bright, noisy truck stops, he'd drunk more coffee while they'd wolfed their food.

Evan had an especially important reason for maintaining this driven schedule though he hadn't had the sleep the other drivers had before beginning this ride. If he arrived back north as early as he anticipated, there'd be the unexpected bonus of a day off and he knew just how he wanted to spend it—who he wanted to spend it with.

He'd been nearly euphoric, on a second wind, when he'd wrapped things up at the mill, showered, shaved and changed his clothes quickly before he set out for Knowle that morning. Once there, he'd stopped first at the Inn, where one of Claire's multitude of cousins was slicing potatoes in the kitchen and informed him that Tess was out and Claire was across the street at Dickie's store. The two of them had their heads together over a magazine when the bell on the store's door alerted them to his arrival.

"Well! Back a bit early, ain't ya?" Dickie had clapped him on the back as Claire's brows raised in surprise while he'd stamped his feet vigorously, blowing into his cupped fists to warm them.

"Just for the day. I've been hauling out-of-state this time and got back earlier than expected, so I got a day off. Thought this might be a nice place to spend it."

He grinned at Claire, who was watching him with knowing eyes. "I gather Tess isn't around?"

"Left here about an hour ago," Dickie broke in to explain. "Borrowed the van to move some things for Rowan. I think she was going to Portland."

Claire turned to face Dickie fully. "Portland? This morning?"

Dickie nodded slowly.

"You're sure?" Her face was growing ashen.

"Taking 'em to one of them—what you call it? Galleries."

It was Evan's turn to study Claire curiously. "He's having an exhibit?"

"I … don't know." She reached to gather the small collection of goods Dickie had bagged for her on the counter. "I've got to get back. Will you be staying the night, Evan, or heading back up north?"

"I should start back tonight, I suppose."

"I'll let Tess know you were here as soon as she gets back," Claire tossed over her shoulder as she dashed out of the store, her mouth a thin line.

"You say she left an hour ago?" Evan asked Dickie as an idea began percolating in his mind.

"About that."

"But she didn't say where she was going?"

"Not the name, no. But someplace downtown. Rowan can tell you, of course."

Rowan would likely also try to talk him into waiting until Tess got back, the most practical choice under the circumstances.

But the last thing he wanted to do was be practical, especially when he'd heard she was in Portland. It just so happened there was something there he'd had his mind on ever since he'd kissed her goodbye. Luck had been very kind to him so far today. He'd take his chances now.

"Got any coffee?" He rubbed at his jaw, wondering if he should stop off at home, then thought better of it.

Dickie poured him a mugful and doused it generously with cream. Dickie never did remember that he preferred his coffee black. "Drive all night, did ya?"

"Just about. Not done yet, though." Evan downed the tepid liquid in a half-dozen swallows and handed the mug back to Dickie. "Thanks a lot."

The old Volvo felt like a limousine after the eighteen-wheeler's plethora of gears and the drive to Portland passed quickly. Though he knew there was the chance he might not find her, he had a good idea where to look.

He didn't have long to wait before he discovered just how accurate his instincts were. He spied the gallery in a square of shops built around a small parking lot. Dickie's van was angling nose-first into a space directly in front of the gallery's double doors.

Evan turned into the parking lot and slowed the car directly behind the parked van, craning forward so he could watch her alight.

Then his jaw dropped as he realized what was happening. The rear of the van had started to loom closer as it rolled directly back toward his car.

He moved to press the car forward an instant too late to prevent what came next.

•

The force of the impact rocked the van in a sickening motion. Tess wrestled the transmission out of reverse and let the van crawl forward.

Mortified, she gathered the shreds of her shattered confidence, trying to remember all the years of driving without mishap as she readied to face the other driver's inevitable outrage.

Rowan's directions had been disjointed. She'd spent at least ten minutes driving in circles around this place, filled with anxiety as she steered Dickie's monolith through the narrow streets. Just as she'd been grateful to find a space directly in front, she'd realized after she pulled into it that unloading the paintings would be far easier if she backed in. She hadn't seen anything behind her when she'd looked, but of course, she hadn't checked all of the mirrors, either.

She caught the barest glimpse of a figure in the side-view mirror now as he leapt from his car—enough to see that he was tall and moving with great speed.

She fumbled for the door handle, her insides sinking, resigned to the fact that this developing nightmare had not yet played out fully.

A pair of palms splayed against the window beside her with a loud thump.

Startled, she turned to meet eyes that danced with familiar light. Her mouth fell open as she cranked down the window and Evan's voice grew louder as the glass wall between them disappeared. "If you don't want me to stay, all you have to do is say so!"

"Evan! How in the ... Where—"

Then she spied the hood of his car behind them. When he opened the van's door, she climbed out and raced toward the back, searching for damage she'd done.

His low soft laugh sounded beside her as he caught hold of her arm. "Right on the bumper, just like you aimed for it."

As she turned toward Dickie's van with a new rush of fear, his voice assured, "Don't worry, a locomotive couldn't dent this." The humor in the eyes that surveyed her was barely suppressed.

"Oh this—thing," she gasped as fear slipped away finally. "I wanted to back it up and I—"

"Could use a little help, I'm sure. It's cantankerous, even when you're used to it." He tucked an arm around her shoulders and guided her toward the car he'd left idling. "You take mine and find a place to park it. I'll see to this."

She was shaking as she climbed in awkwardly and inched the Volvo forward with exaggerated care. She found a space and nosed the car in as though it were made of glass.

As her breathing slowed, random thoughts caught up with her in a tangled noise in her head. What on earth was he doing here? Today, of all days? Oh, God, she had to think. Fast. What would she tell him?

He was bound to notice the paintings stowed in back. Thank heaven Rowan had insisted on wrapping them.

Evan had hoisted himself behind the wheel of Dickie's van and turned it around in three easy moves. His breath made flat clouds in the air as he sauntered toward her.

"Hold on a second." He reached past her and took his gloves and hat from the dashboard then handed her the van's keys and pocketed his own. "There's a sign on the gallery door that says they'll reopen in an hour. I'll help you unload then. But right now, I'm almost as hungry as I am happy to find you. How about some lunch?"

She stared at him, wondering how he'd put everything together so quickly. "When did you get back?"

"Hmm?" he asked as he tugged his gloves on. "Oh. I drove a shipment to Pennsylvania and got back ahead of schedule about six this morning. I ought to be sound asleep, I suppose, but I had too much coffee for that." He stepped forward and closed his arms around her. "Besides, I'd rather be with you than sleep any day."

He kissed her softly, lingeringly, and her apprehension began to disappear. How she had missed him.

She leaned into the warmth of him gratefully. "Have you—talked with Rowan?"

"No. I haven't seen him. I stopped at the Inn long enough to find out you weren't there, so I checked in at Dickie's."

Dickie. Of course. The voice of the Village, keeping everyone up-to-date. But Dickie had known only that she was coming to Portland.

"He didn't know exactly where you were going, of course," Evan answered her thoughts, "but I figured the galleries were all in the same part of town, and I'd know that green monster when I saw it. Even got lucky and found you on the first try."

This was anything but luck. Uneasiness flooded her once again. She'd been growing sure he must already know why she was here, to have found her so easily. It was very difficult to think fast enough to keep up with his caffeinated exuberance. She was the one who seemed to be suffering from sleep deprivation.

"There's a great place for lunch just a few blocks from here. What do you say?"

She couldn't face the thought of eating, though the time would help her think things through. She moved toward the van anxiously.

"All locked up, don't worry. They're safe." Concern crossed his features as he looked at her. "Is everything okay?"

"Fine," she insisted with a smile. "Just recovering from a morning of surprises. Until you arrived, most of them hadn't been very pleasant."

"Let's hope that's changed for the better." He wrapped his arm around her and drew her against him. The contact was a welcome relief that somehow made her feel less alone with this confusion. Her fear had begun to evaporate at the delight of seeing him, yet that sense of something looming at the edges hadn't gone away.

The streets of the city's Old Port were quiet as they moved past the shops in wind that seemed to gnaw at their faces regardless of the direction in which they walked.

Evan touched her sleeve gently as they passed a storefront. "Can we stop in here for a minute?"

"Sure. Anything to keep my ears from falling off in this wind." Tess's eye caught the world "goldsmith" on the wooden sign before they ducked out of the cold.

The store was very small. They had to edge through bulky glass cases filled with an assortment of pendants, earrings, and bracelets.

Evan made his way directly toward the counter in back, where the goldsmith looked up from her work with a quick nod.

Tess was peering at a display of amethyst jewelry when she heard Evan call her name. "Have a look at this."

The jeweler had removed something from the case and placed it in Evan's palm. His eyes were as bright as the shining object he extended toward her. It was a small but elegant diamond set in a gold band that, on closer inspection, Tess saw was a circlet of tiny scallop shells each the size of a snowflake, etched with meticulous detail.

"It's—wonderful." She traced the delicate circumference with her finger.

"Try it on," he urged.

He held the ring between his thumb and index finger.

Swallowing hard, she raised her hand, felt her heart begin to beat faster.

"It's for *this* one," he said with a wry smile and reached for her left hand.

A flush broke over her as the little band slid effortlessly down her ring finger, catching briefly at the knuckle before it settled in place. She was conscious of its unaccustomed weight, astonished at his directness, completely unsure what to do next.

The goldsmith had disappeared into the room behind the counter as if on cue.

Evan watched her face raptly. "What do you think?"

"Evan ..." She breathed his name.

"I've been thinking about it ever since I brought her sign in a few weeks ago and found this. Is it—all right? Obviously, you should have what you really want. If you want to choose something—"

"It's much more than simply all right, Evan!" Tess cut him off.

He regarded her in silence for a few moments. "I hoped you'd like it. And of course that you'd wear it. Eventually. Once—"

"Evan!" She put her fingers to his lips. "One more surprise today and I honestly think I'll swoon away."

His face showed contrition. "I shouldn't have."

She touched his face. "It's absolutely beautiful. It's ... Well, this is a whole new side of you for me. I haven't had a chance to think about anything like this yet."

He leaned forward and kissed her forehead. His sigh brushed past her cheek. "I'm sorry, Tess. Sometimes, I'm just not very good at waiting. Like you said, I can be kind of direct. Maybe too direct."

She worked the ring off her finger and studied it in her palm before handing it back to him. "I can't think of anything I'd rather you be more direct about."

"I'd get down on my knee for this. Though that's probably not such a good idea." His eyes cast around the cramped space.

She nodded and gave him a teasing smile. "I'd have to agree."

His aqua eyes scanned her face for several moments. "Maybe I'm about to embarrass us both."

His shy smile made her think of what he must have looked like as a boy.

"Will you? I mean ... shall we? That is— Will you marry me?"

"I would love to," she said.

The goldsmith's small sounds alerted them that she'd returned to the counter. She checked the ring's size on Tess' finger, then told them she would have it ready in about a week.

They left the shop filled with joy, and stepped out into the cold.

"You know your way around here," Tess observed.

"Yes. I spent a rather difficult year here."

"Really? That long?"

He nodded.

"At the Medical Center?"

"Mostly. I had to stick around for physical therapy, even after I was released. So I took a room down near the park." His lips tightened. "In the candid words of my surgeon, my leg was pretty well smashed to hell."

Tess reached to touch his cheek. "I'm so glad you got through that awful year. You were very brave."

He looked at her for a few moments without saying anything. "Sometimes what looks brave later is simply that you were able to hang on by one thread at a time."

She nodded. "I know."

Her appetite had rallied when they arrived at the restaurant, where the hostess seated them quickly. After they ordered, Tess glanced up and saw a man seated just a few tables away. He was staring hard at them and she looked away quickly.

When the hearty dose of pepper she'd ground into her salad drew a sneeze, she fumbled in her coat pocket for a tissue and again became aware of the man's eyes on her. It was very unnerving and she made a conscious effort not to glance his way again.

"My treat," Evan insisted, when she reached for the bill at the end of the meal.

The man was on his feet, still glaring at them as Tess shrugged on her coat.

Evan excused himself and headed off to find the restroom.

The other man pulled his coat on quickly, tossed several bills on the table, and strode toward the rear of the building without looking at her.

Tess felt a prickling sensation at the back of her neck.

After several long minutes, the man reappeared and hurried toward the door. His dark eyes grazed her face as he passed, and she turned away quickly.

"Let's go." Evan's voice was hoarse as he came along a few seconds later. Her eyes widened in alarm when she saw an angry red blotch on his jaw.

Before she could speak, he moved toward the door with uncharacteristic speed, yanked it open, and stepped aside for her to pass through ahead of him.

Tess glanced around uneasily, but the man was nowhere in sight. "Who was that?" She turned to Evan insistently. "What happened in there?"

"What? Oh, nothing. Don't worry about it." The lines beside his mouth were deep crevices.

"There was a man staring at us all through lunch." She quickened her steps to keep pace with him as he loped ahead. "Please tell me what's wrong, Evan."

He turned apologetically to let her catch up. "It's nothing. Just someone who makes a career out of minding other people's business."

"Why was he so interested in us?"

"Not us. Just me." He set his jaw, then winced at the discomfort it caused. "He's a reporter. He and his buddies had a field day with me after my accident."

His eyes shifted away from her gaze. "He made the mistake of waiting for me outside the room I rented here after I'd just climbed four flights on a leg that had been bullied around in therapy. I believe I asked him politely to get out, though I doubt I gave him enough time to comply before I hauled off and knocked him against the wall."

His face was contrite. "I made a lot of stupid choices in those days. He's waited a long time for that payback."

Tess seized hold of his gloved hand. "I'm so sorry." She touched the mark on his face, which was already fading next to the rising color in his cheeks.

She felt a sudden yearning for this tumultuous day to be over.

"No use dwelling on it," he said.

Bright lights shone from the gallery when they reached the van.

"Listen, I've caused you enough trouble today, and you must need to get back," Tess said as she unlocked the van's rear doors.

"This won't take long," he insisted. "You let them know we're here. I'll start unloading and be right in."

Her mind scanned frantically. Rowan had said the other exhibit would probably still be up. Surely, if she told the owner that Rowan wanted to leave the pieces wrapped until they were to be hung, she and Evan could just drop them quickly and go. Otherwise, she'd run out and tell him the gallery wasn't ready and send him on his way.

Either way, she knew she wanted him away from here as soon as possible.

Chapter 11

The look on Claire's face was like nothing Rowan had ever seen, in all his years of knowing her. Even in the beautiful brashness of her twenties, she'd never looked at him this way. Fierce anger had turned her hazel eyes from their customary tiger's eye hue to a pale olive that reminded him instantly of Celia.

She was shaking visibly, and hadn't even bothered to take off her coat. It was usually a dangerous sign when she strode around without bothering to remove that tartan jacket that made her stand out so brightly in the snow.

"You gave me your word!" Her tone was outraged. "Said you'd wait until we could be sure that this wouldn't trouble anyone, especially Evan!"

Rowan watched her flushed face warily. "What are you talking about?"

"If you play stupid with me, I swear—how could you be so selfish?" She wrenched the coat off impatiently and tossed it on a chair.

Claire in a rage of righteousness unsettled him more than a little. And he'd felt so sure he wouldn't have to go through any of this. He sighed, then swallowed hard against the uneasiness rising in his throat. It would be very important to remember where she was softest, and be sure to use it.

"How could you involve her in this? Did you help her understand just how he's likely to feel about what she's doing for you today?" Claire's eyes, really green now, were making his heart ache as they became unbearably familiar in a way he hadn't thought of in some time.

"Tess? Well, yes. I ... merely suggested that she forgo discussing it until it was all … accomplished." Rowan struggled to deal with the words she was hurling at him and piece together an answer that would buy him time.

"Then what was she supposed to do? Drop it into casual conversation?"

"Things will evolve on their own, somehow. I suppose I'll bring it up to him, in time." Rowan wiped his brush on a rag as he looked at her. "It seemed like the perfect opportunity with him away. I didn't tell you because I knew you'd get upset like this."

"I trusted you. Believed that you could overlook your own ideas and ambitions just once. Could have some patience."

"There isn't enough time as it is, can't you see that?" he cut her off angrily. "You'd have let them molder there for all eternity if she hadn't bought the place and you hadn't had to find somewhere else to keep them."

She watched him in a silence that was more unsettling than her anger.

"Claire, don't you care about her work? Doesn't it matter to you at all?" He was sorry now, that he'd been so short with her. But he knew he was going to have to push this point firmly. She had been impossibly stubborn and uncooperative about this.

"I hope you've thought very carefully about what you'll say to him," Claire said. "Because I don't think you'll have long to wait for that opportunity."

"Whatever do you mean?"

"I don't know which one of us was the more surprised when Dickie mentioned where Tess had gone this morning," Claire told him.

"He was here?" Rowan breathed, aghast.

"He was, and you'd better pray he was discouraged enough at missing Tess that he turned right around and headed back up north."

"Claire …" He reached for her hand, but she pulled it away. Rowan squared his shoulders and told her defensively, "He's going to have to deal with this sooner or later. This work is too important."

"More important to you than his feelings, obviously."

"You can't believe that. You'd be the first to admit that he can't go on avoiding something just because it's going to hurt him to face it, finally. He's got an excellent opportunity for happiness now.

Surely that will help him deal with this."

"It might have, given enough time." She shook her head. "How could you do this to Tess?"

Rowan waved a hand dismissively. "She wanted to help. Don't worry, I'm the one to blame, and either way, he'll forgive her anything."

"How easy do you think it is to forgive when you've felt betrayed by practically everyone?" Her voice was filled with weary sadness. "Why didn't you wait?"

"I didn't want to waste any more time."

"You didn't want to wait to have what you want. You never have, any more than you've learned how to want what you have."

Her disappointment was palpable, weighting the air around them.

Rowan's eyes narrowed. "Would it be preferable that I should consistently acquiesce, as you have?" His gaze accused her. "You never had it in you to own her, as I did."

"Neither of us owned her, Rowan," Claire said quietly. "It was made clear to us early on that the consequence of our choices wasn't ever going to be something we could own."

Her eyes brimmed with tears, but her voice remained steady. "What I did do was to keep my promise to those who helped me."

"Your sister," he snorted derisively. "And that lout of a husband of hers. Meddling bunch of—"

"Her parents, Rowan," Claire interrupted firmly. "More parents to her than you and I ever were."

He looked away quickly.

"I did much more than 'own' her, Rowan. I gave her up so that she could have some sort of life, though it almost killed me. I lived through realizing that the night we made her was probably the last time I'd ever see you again."

Tears were moving slowly down Claire's pink cheeks. "And then, I had to stick around to watch her grow up; become confused; ask me for answers I couldn't give her. And finally, I had to watch her break the heart of the only other person who ever really loved her, and my own heart broke too."

She reached for her coat slowly. "You wonder how I could hold her work back, but you really wouldn't understand if I told you. But he will." Claire's chin bobbed confidently. "God, help me, if it's the last thing I do, I'll make him understand that I'd have dashed those paintings to pieces if it would make up one little bit for the pain she caused him."

•

Rowan sat in silence after the door slammed behind her, wreathed with remorse. Why hadn't he believed her when she'd asserted that it was too soon? It was true, what she had said about his impatience. All his life he had shown a relentless persistence in acquiring what he wanted.

At forty, with his marriage in shambles, he had wanted Claire for a fitting culmination to an idyllic summer. He winced as he remembered the words with which she'd described for him the pain that had caused her, feelings she'd never shared with him until now. Feelings of which he'd been wholly unaware.

At fifty, he had seen the zenith of his career, at the expense of his marriage and his wife's substantial inheritance. And finally, he realized, at the cost of her life.

Then, in Knowle, he had discovered Celia, had known from the first that she was his, and had invested all of his energy in cultivating her undeniable genius, allying himself with Evan, to ensure that the bond would tighten.

Her death had been a shattering blow to his vicarious pursuits and he had consoled himself with the dream that he would see that her work survived her and triumphed as his own had failed to do.

Yes, all his life he had reached beyond his grasp, had been proud of it. But he wasn't proud now. For the first time, he understood that he had pushed too far.

•

Tess's heart hammered as she stepped through the gallery's double doors and noted with quick relief that the white walls were still covered with paintings—huge, garish abstracts that struck her as particularly hideous.

"May I help you?" A man with shoulder-length hair and a brilliant diamond in his ear greeted her lazily.

She explained who she was and what she had brought, and he instructed her to line the pieces up against the wall as he wouldn't be hanging them until the next day.

She released the breath she'd been holding in a grateful sigh, pleased that something would go right today after all.

Evan appeared inside the door and set two paintings down where she gestured. Together, they made numerous trips back and forth to the van, handling the packages carefully.

"Last two," he told her cheerfully as he slammed the van doors shut and reached to take one from her. "See? That didn't take long at all." She held the glass door for him. "How many are there all together?"

"About twenty."

"Really? Why so few?"

As she was formulating her answer, a voice shrilled through the room, and Tess's heart sank.

"Evan!" A woman with multi-colored streaks in her tousled hair teetered toward him on stiletto heels. Bracelets made a noisy symphony on the arms she threw around him in a swirl of peacock silk and musky perfume. "Nobody said a word about this."

The man with the earring looked up then continued reading his magazine.

"Marielle ..." Evan's face was an uneasy mask of surprise.

The woman seemed to take proprietorship of him as she faced him, squaring her back to Tess, who had to step away to avoid the dancing spears of her heels. The throaty voice was a languid drawl. "They told me you'd been chased away by all that hounding and drama. But I never believed it for a minute. I knew you much better than that."

Her voice was ripe with implied meaning as a hand with fuchsia nails explored his sleeve in a caress. "Still the same beautiful Evan. The years must have been especially kind to you, to make up for everything."

His jaw tightened as his questioning eyes met Tess's over her head.

Tess felt the world sliding away from under her feet. The hanger wire of the painting she held began to cut into her flesh.

She staggered backward awkwardly and set the painting against the wall.

"I had no idea—this is your gallery?"

She answered with a triumphant nod that tossed her curiously colored hair. "We opened about a year ago. We've had some good things, but I expect this exhibit to be a kind of turning point. Especially if you're—"

"You should talk to Tess about this," he broke in. "She's in charge of these."

Marielle turned and acknowledged her, finally, as Evan introduced them.

The pale blue eyes swept over her quickly. "Did you know Celia, too?"

The name pierced Tess like an arrow as she forced a stranger's voice past the constriction in her throat. "No, we never met. I think everything should be all set here. Rowan said he'd call today, in case you have any questions."

The furrow between Evan's brows deepened as he watched them.

"What about the bios?" Marielle wondered. "Did you bring the bios?"

Tess nodded woodenly. "They're in the van. I'll just go—"

"Let me," Evan was already halfway to the door. "I saw the box on the seat. I should have brought it in." He disappeared outside before she could speak.

Marielle eyed her curiously as a spring inched the door shut with a low whine. "Is he coming to the opening?"

"No, I don't think ..." Tess groped for quick words to explain, urge Marielle not to mention Celia again. "It's really better not to ask him about this."

Through the glass, she saw Evan emerge from the van with the ream-sized box cradled in his arm.

"Rowan didn't plan on him ... coming." Tess's voice froze when she saw him lift the top of the box to check the contents.

Then a lump rose like a fist in her throat as she watched him replace the cover with infinite care. His lined face spoke worlds as he limped toward the door.

Tess was rooted to the floor, longing for it to open and swallow her, during the interminable moments before he appeared inside. She could feel his gaze burning into her as she averted her own helplessly.

His voice was deadly calm as he handed the box to Marielle. "I'd like to have a look at these, if you don't mind."

"The paintings? Go right ahead." She gestured graciously and threw Tess a look that clearly discounted the concerns she'd expressed. "I'll get some scissors."

A loud ripping sound halted her in her tracks.

Marielle's eyes widened as she watched Evan wrench the thick wrappings open as though all of his emotion was focused in his hands, exposing one painting after another with a single powerful tear.

Tess finally stole a look at him as he peeled the covering back to reveal the self-portrait of Celia. The muscles in his arms and shoulders tensed visibly.

"Breathtaking, wasn't she?" Marielle shot Tess a knowing look. "No one else could ever come close, could they, Evan?"

He looked like a man on the eve of his execution as he stood before the portrait.

Marielle clattered over and brushed against him. "You'll be here? For the opening? It only seems right."

"I'm afraid that won't be possible." His voice had deepened. His features remained frozen.

Marielle took several steps backward. Her eyes flashed to Tess uncertainly. "Oh, well. That's too bad. Of course, if you've—"

"Where did they come from?" Evan's eyes dismissed her as they turned on Tess.

"They were in the attic. At the Spinnaker." She felt like a thief caught in the act. She wanted to describe Rowan's plans, but his expression made it difficult to speak. "They're so—wonderful. It seemed wrong to keep them there ..." Her voice trailed off as she realized she was condemning herself with each word.

For an instant, she saw the unbelieving hurt in his eyes before they glazed over icily, like polished stones. "Yes. Of course."

He turned toward the paintings, his look more a grimace than a smile. "Mustn't hide them away, certainly. The net result of showing them will far outweigh any—cost—involved, won't it?" His voice broke off at these last words, as her betrayal stared back at her from his eyes.

Pain knifed her heart. Her thoughts moved toward him, but her body remained riveted to the floor, and still no words would come as she floundered in this sea of confusion that was swallowing her.

Oh God, why hadn't Rowan told her the most important thing about Marielle? How had she failed to understand just how badly Evan would react to this?

The zipper of his parka made an abrupt sound as he yanked

it upward then dragged his left leg toward the door with long, impatient strides.

"I'd say you're all set here." He gave her one last glimpse of his tortured eyes before he disappeared through the door with angry haste.

Tess couldn't will herself either to move or look at Marielle, so consumed was she with the whirlwind of this awful scene.

The sound of a telephone chirruped and Marielle teetered past Tess as though she were a piece of sculpture, intent on making the most of this timely interruption.

When Tess finally pushed out the door after him, the Volvo was turning up dust at the far end of the parking lot as he spun the wheel in his hands with uncharacteristic speed and was gone.

She staggered toward the van, fumbling in her pocket for the keys and barely made it into the driver's seat before she gave way to a storm of tears and hurt confusion. As she collapsed against the steering wheel, the sense of doom that had stalked her all day had its way at last.

Chapter 12

Claire and two helpers were moving hurriedly around the kitchen when Tess returned. Her head throbbed with a dull ache as she took off her coat and stumbled toward the stove. "Where do you need help most?"

Claire turned at the sound of her voice and strode across the kitchen to enfold her wordlessly in a sturdy hug. "There's not so many we can't manage. Why don't you—"

"I'm sorry I've run so late." Tess turned toward the dining room abruptly. "They must need help with tables."

Claire took her arm. "Honey, I don't think—"

But before she could finish, Tess had bolted through the swinging door and moved to where Claire's cousin was pouring glasses of water at the hutch.

After greeting diners at two of the tables and taking their orders, Tess hurried back to the kitchen and set to work. She moved numbly through the rush of the dinner hour, drawing on every last ounce of inner strength to keep things moving, chatting mindlessly with customers, trying to put as much distance as possible between this world and the scene at the gallery.

Funny, how easy it could be when there was so much to do. Just like tending to needs at the hospital when patients demanded help from six directions and all she'd been able to think about was how soon Andy's surgery would be finished, or whether he'd be able to escape into more than two hours of sleep before she brought more morphine. She seemed to find endless reserves from which to draw for others when her own pain was strongest.

Several parties of weekend guests arrived and Tess replaced Claire in the refuge of the kitchen, freeing her to assist them. It was past nine when the other helpers finally went home and they had the kitchen to themselves as the door to the dining room swung shut behind Claire.

Tess looked up from where she sat at the table, her head on her folded arms.

Claire pulled a chair near her. "Rowan's called several times." She exhaled slowly. "I've told him the delivery was made, and he'll have to wait to know more."

"I don't know what to tell him." Tess shook her head as tears welled in her eyes.

"You don't have to tell him anything. He's the one who's got explaining to do." Claire's jaw tightened. She fumbled in her oversized apron pocket, brought forth a clump of crumpled tissues and handed them to Tess. Her own eyes were red-rimmed.

"And I have, too. That's for sure." She reached for Tess's hand. "He found you, didn't he?"

Tess nodded.

"Dickie had a feeling that's where he was so determined to go. I prayed he was wrong." After a pause, she asked, "He—saw the paintings?"

"Oh yes," Tess said bitterly. "He saw them all right."

Claire let a few seconds of silence go by, then asked, "And he's gone back up north?"

Tess shrugged helplessly. "I don't know where he's gone."

Claire grasped the thin shoulders and turned Tess to face her. "You've done nothing wrong, do you understand?" Claire's expression was as insistent as her tone. "Whatever this has stirred up is nothing you're responsible for, and I don't want you to forget that."

"He looked so ... hurt," Tess sobbed out finally, remembering the sweetness of the time with Evan in Portland, before the shock of the revelations at the gallery. "I never imagined—why didn't Rowan tell me?"

"Tess, you're caught in the middle of something that's never been right." Tears sprang quickly in Claire's eyes and she dabbed at them with a tissue.

"Rowan has been determined to do this ever since she died and I've resisted it as long as I could." She drew a breath. "Don't you ever wonder why Celia's work is so important to him?"

Tess shook her head, confused. "He was obviously very fond of her. The paintings are so beautiful. It must frustrate him that she didn't live to get the recognition she deserved. It only seems natural he'd want to help. I imagine you must feel the same way. She was part of your family."

"She was part of his, too," Claire said quietly.

Tess stared back at her. "Rowan? I don't understand. How could she be?"

"She was our daughter." Claire's face was a mask of sadness. "The part of him he left behind the summer he first came here. The only part I had—the one I couldn't keep."

"You weren't her—aunt?"

"No. It was her aunt who raised her."

"Claire," Tess breathed. "Didn't Rowan know?"

"Not until it was too late to make any difference. He'd gone back to New York before I even knew what had happened. I had no idea how to find him, how to go about telling him, even if I did. He had a wife and a family of his own. I knew he'd have no room in his life for me, for us. This was the only home, the only work I knew. There weren't many choices then, and I'd have had her, either way.

"I let my family tell me what to do. I didn't know any better. They never knew who her father was. My sister's husband couldn't have children, and the way seemed clear—and at least I'd be able to see her. Be part of her life."

"They raised her?"

"Yes. And their lives finally got full enough that they forgot about the thing they were never going to forgive me for. I went away, of course, so no one would know. That's what you did in those days. And they adopted their baby girl when I came back. They were adamant that she must never know the truth."

Claire paused and blew her nose, then continued, "When she was fourteen, Rowan came back. Don't ask me how, but he knew whose child she really was from the first time Evan brought her there. Evan was the only one who ever gave her work any encouragement. My family thought such things were sheer folly, a waste of time."

Tess was watching Claire's face as though she'd never seen it before. She reached across the table and laced her fingers into her hand. "You must have been happy to see him again."

"I was too shocked to feel anything but fear. I had everything I could do to make him leave things alone. Actually, I was angry that he'd come back and wanted to stir things up. I couldn't see that he had any right. But I could see he loved her, in his way. He loved what he saw of himself in her, anyway. We found a way to live with it as it was. He was all set to get her work into a gallery in Boston when she died. He was devastated."

Tess sighed. "However have you managed?"

"I don't know. I spent years telling myself how different it might have been. But even the person who loved her more than any of us couldn't seem to make it any better."

"Then why would an exhibit of her work upset him so?" Tess wondered. "Especially if he cared so much about it?"

"I imagine he dreads the thought because it'll bring the whole thing up again—his fall. That terrible accident. I don't know how to begin to describe how bad it was for Evan afterward, Tess. He had taken care of her in ways that are ... complicated to understand.

"There was always a streak of something restless in Celia that nothing would satisfy. As she got older, it became clear something was wrong. There were terrible highs when she'd do just what she pleased and Evan would pick up the pieces behind her. Then came the lows, and surely, he's the only reason she got through as many of them as she did. She was awful to him, at times." Claire blinked hard in memory. "Absolutely humiliated him. He stuck by her through all of it, then not only lost her, but had to face everyone's ugly accusations, especially my family's."

She balled the tissue she held in her fist. "I should have been more outspoken. I never stood up to any of them any more than my mother ever did."

"Why would people think he'd killed her?" Tess asked. "Surely they saw how much he loved her?"

Instantly, memory stabbed her with the realization that this man who'd been so kind, who she'd come to love, might never want to see her again.

"The night before she died, there was going to be a dance here at the Spinnaker. It was supposed to be a sort of rehearsal party for their wedding that weekend. That afternoon, my sister told me that Celia had been seeing someone else during the months while Evan had been away overseas and was probably going to call the wedding off. She couldn't wait to tell me, really. She and my brother-in-law never cared much for Evan, but they were delighted with the new prospect, especially because he 'came from money.'

"I nearly died when I found out who it was. Celia showed up here with him that night. That's how poor Evan found out ..." Claire's voice broke off as she remembered.

"She paraded him around, displaying him for everyone to see." Claire's voice caught again as she wiped her eyes. "It was Stephen Kearsage."

Tess gasped. "Not ..."

"Rowan's youngest son, yes."

"Didn't Rowan know?"

"Celia had managed to keep that quiet. She knew how much Rowan cared for Evan, and Rowan was still too much of an asset to her career plans to alienate."

Claire shook her head slowly. "I don't know what would have happened to Rowan if he'd found out, but he never did. I protected him from that."

"And Celia never knew?" Tess wondered aloud softly.

"Ah, dear," Claire sighed deeply. "You know, there's nothing in life that doesn't catch up with you, if you try to keep things hidden."

Tess squeezed her hand, nodding her understanding.

"I probably should never have done it, but there was no one else who could. And it had to be done. Celia couldn't wait to flaunt Stephen in Evan's face, and everyone could see how upset he was. Maybe that's what pushed me to do it. I took her aside after both men left the inn that night and told her the truth about who her parents were. I should have known better, of course."

Claire paused, her unfocused gaze on the hands she'd folded in her lap. "She was already—manic—that night, and I ought to have figured she'd run to Evan, and that no matter how angry he was, he'd still try to take care of her.

"God forgive me, I should never have let her go to him that way. In my heart, I've always known that he was too perceptive not to be aware of the real situation all along. I've never doubted that he was trying to save her that night, and that his silence hasn't only been to keep her secret, but mine. Ours."

"Do you think she ..." Tess didn't know how to phrase her question.

"I've spent more nights trying to figure out what happened, but there's no being sure really. When someone found the two of them on the beach the next morning, people drew their own conclusions."

Tess felt dazed as she took this in.

"I've poured far too much out on you after the day you've had," Claire apologized. "But you have to understand that you've done nothing wrong. In a way, I think you're Providence's way of helping us all begin to get past this, once and for all."

She sighed heavily as she rose to her feet and smoothed the folds of her skirt. "I've asked all three of the girls to come back tomorrow afternoon to be here for dinner. I'd like to take some time for an obligation that's waited much too long."

Tess leapt to her feet to press her cheek against Claire's.

"Take all the time you want."

•

The cloud of smoke in the room was smarting Evan's eyes, or maybe it was tears that were doing that, and that wouldn't do at all. He dragged his sleeve across his face and reached for the bottle whose contents were dwindling. He sneered at himself and the cliché of this choice, but he was pursuing it with determination just the same.

He'd never had much stomach for liquor, but he wasn't trying to please his palate. What his mind was demanding was numbness, preferably blackness. A dark retreat, as the morphine had been during those days when he hadn't been able to understand why he didn't die, not so much from the pain in his body as from that in his heart.

He had positioned himself with his back to the room in the low-ceilinged tavern, whose dark log walls and dim lighting created a sense of permanent nighttime. Some of his coworkers still cast curious glances his way, but however surprised they were to see him, they'd quickly sensed he wasn't here for social reasons and left him alone.

He had hoped there'd be another rig for him to take on a long haul when he'd got back here last night and been dejected to discover there was no work for him until morning. He'd spent a useless night without any possibility of sleep and had finally walked for hours until the protest in his leg distracted him from some of his anguish.

Each time his thoughts finally backed off from the shock of seeing Celia's paintings, the fact that it was Tess who'd brought them there, he remembered that God-blasted reporter whose byline now ran with stories about the arts.

At daylight, he'd thrown himself into ten long hours at the mill only to discover that even physical exhaustion didn't silence the endless narrative in his mind.

That was when he'd decided that this course of action was merited, maybe even therapeutic, though his first few shots only served to remind him how vile he really found this. With persistence, he'd reached a point where his sight was growing fuzzy at the edges. There was warmth in his gut that held the promise of sleep, and the increasing spans during which he seemed able to think of nothing at all were heartening.

He felt light pressure on his shoulder, worlds away, and turned to see the tall, angular figure standing beside him. Through the blear in his eyes, the sight of her auburn hair made something seize in his throat.

The hazel eyes watching him began to weave in a disconcerting motion and, with every ounce of energy he had left, he sprang to his feet and staggered past her, certain there wouldn't be time to reach the restroom before his body drew the line at his abuse.

He was thankful his muted consciousness made it all seem over before it began as he bathed his face in icy water from the tap at the sink in the squalid men's room afterward. Funny, it wasn't a men's room, he supposed. There certainly wasn't any women's room to distinguish it as such.

Someone was swinging a sledgehammer back and forth behind his eyes as he groped his way back out again and slumped into the chair.

Claire was perched on the bench across the table from him and he eyed her sheepishly, grimacing at the taste in his mouth.

"Is this helping?" She regarded the bottle of bourbon doubtfully.

"Well, you know what they say. Put a bottle in front of me, if I can't have a frontal lob—" A ragged cough abruptly shook his body. When it was over, he gave a half-grin, then winced as a twinge stabbed at his temple. "Trouble is, I can't even seem to get drunk right."

"You'll thank yourself in the morning."

"Morning might as well be right now, for all the sleep I'm getting."

He leveled his gaze on her and the two of them sat in silence for a few long moments. The liquor that had departed his system so rapidly had left just the faintest sense of ease. His head was beginning to feel better now, as his vision cleared.

She seemed completely improbable, sitting so straight and thoughtful in this God-awful place. How ludicrous that she should be sitting across from him here, nearly as ludicrous as the fact he was almost glad to see her. Maybe he finally had fallen asleep.

"Like anything?" He gestured toward the bar expansively.

"I'd like to talk with you."

"Really? I thought maybe you'd come up for the floor show." He smirked. "I may be it, tonight."

"Perhaps I should wait ..." she hesitated.

"Oh, no! I'm all ears!" he insisted, his smile sardonic. "Don't let my present circumstances discourage you. I've done everything I can to lose consciousness and this is what I get." He shook his head. "I get the damnedest results these days."

"Maybe you're in the wrong place."

"Maybe I'm in the wrong life." His voice boomed on this last word and others' heads looked up toward the table.

Claire studied him quietly. "Someone doesn't think so."

"And just who might that be?"

"Someone who loves you the way you deserve to be loved."

"Really? I'd say she's got plenty of other things keeping her busy. Venturing into the art world. Brings back old memories in a way." His eyes narrowed, glittering as they met hers then and he declared, "Just what I don't need."

"She had nothing to do with it, Evan," Claire said. "She just got caught in the middle. She had no idea what she was getting into."

"Well, I imagine she has now."

"How's she supposed to understand any of it, when you've told her nothing?"

He averted his eyes quickly from the truth of her accusation.

"You can't blame her—you mustn't. Whatever she did came from a sincere desire to do something she imagined you'd want, based on how little she knows about the situation."

Claire's gaze was insistent as he met it reluctantly. "It was all his idea. Surely you know that. You know as well as anyone why it's always been so important to him."

Evan couldn't believe what she appeared to be telling him as he stared at her. "Do I?"

She seemed to hesitate before she said, "We both know you do. But none of it's any excuse for what you've put yourself through. It never has been. Any more than there's any excuse for the wrongs I've committed against you. You did everything in your power to help Celia. You had to see it was hopeless. Whatever happened that night, it's time to let it go. There are no more secrets to keep. Tess surely understands it all better for knowing that, now."

Surprise must have been plain on his face as he struggled to take in her words. "You—you've told her? About … Celia?"

A lump filled his throat. He'd said her name. Aloud.

Something was wrenching again at his insides, but not nausea, this time. Pain. "About—"

"Yes. I've told her what I should have told you a long time ago, though I've guessed you were smart enough to figure it out on your own. Now it's time for you to finally let go of it and trust Tess enough to share your pain. To stop blaming yourself for what you couldn't change, and find the happiness you deserve."

He drew back slightly as he looked at her, as his next words rose like bile in his throat. "The happiness I deserve?" His tone was ironic. "You think I should just … put it all behind me now, do you?"

"I think it's time, yes."

He laughed bitterly. Then his face sobered. "Believe me, the best thing is for me to back out right now. Without burdening her with the ugly explanations that, I promise you—" He leaned forward, his tone rising. "—will make her want to get as far away from me as she can."

Claire stared at him, eyes wide. "Surely you can't have such little faith in her! If so, then I've misjudged you badly."

She continued firmly, "I've watched you lose one thing after another and stand up to it. Face it, you chose to love someone who didn't know how to love anyone. It wasn't your fault. If that left you so scared of love that you'd throw this chance with Tess away, then you're not the man I thought you were."

The eyes across from him were now the same pale green that had so often flashed in Celia's and their familiarity was a spear in his heart that prodded his anger forward.

"If you knew what I really am, you wouldn't let me near her." His voice was a deadly hiss of disgust.

Claire's mouth gaped as he leapt to his feet, wrenched a handful of bills from his pocket and threw them on the table.

"Evan—what are you—" She rose quickly and hurried after him as he loped toward the door.

A dozen pair of curious eyes followed them.

She seized his arm as she caught up with him outside. "How long are you going to keep running away?"

His features were rigid in the flickering red neon of the sign overhead. "I killed her. Do you understand? Just as sure as if I'd thrown her off that cliff. In fact, that might have been kinder than what it was I actually did."

The clouds of his labored breathing swirled around them.

Claire's eyes blinked rapidly as she watched him.

"Evan ... Whatever happened?"

"There is nothing to justify what I did," he told her. "But don't worry. The justice is that I can't possibly run away from it."

Then he spun on his heel and left her to watch him retreat into the night.

Chapter 13

Claire, Rowan and Tess attended the opening of the exhibit of Celia's work at Tess' insistence.

She had waited up for Claire the night the older woman had gone to find Evan, watching the hours tick by. Claire's sad face had told her everything when she returned.

The following day, a visit from Matthew Crane's family had brought Tess clearer understanding of just what Evan was dreading about the exhibit of Celia's paintings. When the Cranes had come to the inn for dinner that evening, Matthew had run into the kitchen enthusiastically to announce that, "Evan's picture is in the newspaper."

Claire had nodded solemnly from where she'd stood at the stove.

When Tess had gone out to greet the Cranes and take their order, Matthew's father had brought the matter up with a hint of surprise in his voice. "We had no idea he'd been involved in something like that? Did you?"

Tess had also noted with hurt disappointment the guarded expression his wife had worn at the mention of the man who had, just weeks before, acted in an instant to save their son's life.

Later that night, Tess, found the Inn's copy of the Portland paper where Claire had deliberately made it scarce. The generous half-page article spelled out the details of Evan's and Celia's fall most explicitly and although Tess didn't know the writer's name, she imagined she'd have recognized his face in an instant.

The gallery had apparently hung Celia's self-portrait and the one of Evan side-by-side and the writer had written a review that emphasized the artist's tragic history and featured photographs of these same two paintings.

Tess's heart sank when she saw this.

She had resolved then that they would go to Portland, although convincing Claire hadn't been easy. No doubt she had finally agreed only to please Tess.

When Tess had gone to see Rowan for the first time since her trip to the gallery, his expression and demeanor, both usually so lively, had shown that he was more than paying the price for his decision. Any joy the exhibit's success might have given him had been rubbed out by the anger and pain it had caused. He reminded Tess of a repentant child, eager to make up in any small way for an unforgivable act.

Claire's anger had cooled at last to the point where Tess could get the three of them to talk together, and the decision was made.

They were silent on the drive to Portland, Helmut's windshield wipers making a steady slap like a pair of parentheses, meeting and parting in the light, wet snow.

The gallery hosted a substantial crowd that night, despite the weather.

Marielle was dressed in a floor-length dress of crimson wool that was cut provocatively low at the neck, where large garnets glittered in a necklace with an Art-Deco setting. She greeted Rowan in a rush of enthusiasm, remembered to acknowledge Tess and Claire, then left them alone to make her rounds.

An oblong table was spread with platters of hors d'oeuvres and silver trays of glasses whose champagne sparkled in the gallery lights.

The paintings looked wonderful, each a brilliant world of color all its own, and the room buzzed with conversation and laughter.

Tess wandered around slowly, taking in each canvas with deep concentration.

When she overheard voices speculating about Evan near the portrait of him, she moved away, and felt a quick spasm near her heart. He wouldn't fit into this scene very well at all, she realized suddenly, any more than she did, than Claire did.

Her gaze found the older woman where she stood alone before a small still life in a corner, which showed a spiraling seashell near its base. She was dressed in the deep green wool suit that only appeared at weddings and funerals, and occasionally, church. Her auburn hair had been freshly coiffed at Patti's Village Beauty Nook and there were tiny pearls in her earlobes. Tess felt a sudden rush of love as she watched her.

Rowan was strolling slowly from painting to painting with his cane, shoulders stooped, white hair bright under the lights.

Tess watched as he drew near Claire and stood beside her.

She gave him her hand when he reached for it, and they stood together, apart from the others.

Then a dark-haired man in a sports coat and tie approached them, his head bobbing animatedly, hands gesturing as he talked. It was the man from the restaurant, Tess realized—the reporter.

A few moments later, his eyes darted across to where she watched him as Claire and Rowan moved away from him slowly.

Tess turned in the direction of the restroom as he strode briskly toward her across the polished floor. Within seconds, he appeared in front of her, obstructing her path. The dark eyes peered down his angular nose at her. "Haven't I seen you before?"

Is there a ruder way to approach someone? she wanted to snap. She tipped her head back and met his gaze. "I don't know. Have you? I don't recall being introduced."

"I think I have," he nodded confidently. "I believe you were with Evan Marston at the time."

She shrugged indifferently. "Perhaps I was."

His smile was tight and businesslike as he finally gave her his name. Anger rose in a hot flash as she heard it and looked away without volunteering her own.

"He's not here," the man noted.

Her jaw tightened as she glanced at him, then scanned the room deliberately. "No, he doesn't appear to be, does he?"

"Isn't he coming?"

"I wouldn't know."

The man's eyes narrowed with what looked like disappointment as he watched her. "I suppose he wouldn't come."

"Oh, do you know him?" She deliberately kept her tone light, infusing surprise into her voice as she tossed this out.

His smile was thin and sharp. "You might say that." He slid a hand into his pocket, turning away slightly to gesture toward the paintings. "I don't suppose he'd want any part of this."

Her face was impassive. "No, I'd say his part in all this is finished."

His features registered surprise. "What can you tell me about what he's doing now?"

Tess felt delighted to respond in an almost casual tone with the very first words that came to her mind. "Absolutely nothing." *And that's even the truth*, her thoughts added sadly.

He hovered closer. "Really, I'd just like to ask you a few questions, if you don't mind ..."

She definitely didn't want to continue this conversation, felt growing outrage at his probing.

Her eyes shot up at him quickly. "About what?" she challenged. A light sweat was beginning to form at the backs of her knees.

"About him, of course. I plan to write a follow-up story about the exhibit. It wouldn't seem complete without a little history."

"I'm afraid I can't help you." She turned to move away, but he still blocked her path.

"Can you tell me how I might reach him?"

Her tone was angry now. "No, I can't."

"Look," he maintained his stance, directly in front of her. "I just want to get the facts straight."

She drew herself up to her full height and glared at him, then, barely able to keep from screaming. "If you want to get the facts straight," she spoke slowly, her tone low and terse, "then you'd better stick to covering the exhibit and the artist. Anything else would be—irrelevant, really." She tossed her head, as though bored, then turned to glare at him. "Or even downright invasive."

His eyes showed his surprise, and he stepped aside as she pushed first against, then past him to go find the others.

As the three of them took one final look around, Claire asked, "Did that miserable pondscum give you any trouble?"

Tess smiled sweetly. "Oh, not at all. Especially once he understood that I'd be absolutely no help to him."

Tess noticed that Rowan's shoulders were sagging and his face was lined with fatigue. "I think we've paid our very best respects here tonight. Shall we go home?" she offered, and they both nodded eagerly.

Snow was coming down in big wet flakes when they reached the car.

The older couple discussed the paintings for a long while

afterward in muted voices as Tess drove. Each canvas sparked recollection of things long forgotten, buried, since the canvasses had been stored away in the Spinnaker's attic.

One vivid landscape had spoken to Rowan of a happy event. Meticulous still lifes had drawn forth memories of troubled times for Claire, ones she had once thought would never pass. Then Rowan's handkerchief had been passed forward from the back seat, to capture Claire's quiet tears.

The atmosphere in the car grew tense and silent when the outside lane of the turnpike became too covered with a slick white coating for travel. Tess dropped Helmut's speed lower as the headlights carried less and less into the blinding whiteout spawned by swirling clouds of snow.

Scores of taillights glowed from the breakdown lane as drivers yielded to the increasing storm. Tess's heart felt very full in her chest as she drove on steadily, closing the distance to Knowle, determined to get back to familiar surroundings.

It was Claire who mentioned Evan, hesitantly, inquiring if Rowan had heard anything.

The old man sighed, gazing out at the fields as they entered the outskirts of the village. "I think he was at the boathouse most of the afternoon. I saw his car from the studio."

Tess felt a sudden swimming sensation in her midsection. "He's back?" she asked, her voice catching a bit in her throat as she did.

"Yes," Rowan confirmed. "I don't know how long it's been. I've seen the car for the past two days."

"What's he doing there?"

"There's an old sloop of his father's he keeps there. He's working on that, I'd suppose."

"And you haven't seen him?"

"No," Rowan's voice was heavy. "Though I'd hoped to."

Tess knew then that she wasn't going back to the Inn.

Rowan's house was dark when they arrived. The two women helped him get settled comfortably before they left.

The snowplows were just starting out and the slippery streets were slick under the tires as Tess nudged the car through the mounting accumulation in the Inn's lot. She left the motor running and made no effort to get out.

Claire turned to her, surprised. "Aren't you coming in?"

Tess shook her head.

"It's bad," Claire admonished. "Can't it wait?"

"I can't," Tess told her. "Not another day longer."

Claire nodded. "I suppose you can't. Please, please be careful." She caught hold of Tess's gloved hand. "I could come with you. Alicia would gladly stay, if I asked her."

"I'll be fine. Don't worry."

She watched as Claire climbed out and picked her way up the snow-covered steps. She raised her hand in a wave as Tess turned the wheel and steered the car out of the lot.

The wheels spun for purchase on the slushy streets. Out near the shore, the road all but disappeared and she fought to follow it, anxiety riding her nerves, making her shoulders ache with tension.

She'd spent many winters on worse roads and knew the feelings churning inside were about what was ahead of her at Evan's rather than any fear about the storm.

It didn't matter any more, what he did or didn't do. All that mattered was the emotion she had seen in Claire's face as she'd studied the paintings, Rowan's quiet regret, and the feeling, growing stronger by the minute that they had all done the right thing.

Claire and Rowan deserved this effort, after all that they had survived, and she had a right of her own to face Evan and see how this could be resolved. If it meant the end of what she'd had with him, it must at least mean that the ties that bound him to the others would only be strengthened by the trial that had tested them.

She had to try and show him her belief in him, and love for him, regardless of the rejection it might bring. If he chose to remain a prisoner of the things that plagued him, she had to know she'd made every effort to invite him away from that.

A snow plow loomed out of the sheet of white and passed her, its winking lights quickly becoming tiny sparks in the distance. She wondered if the driver had even seen her.

Then her car began sliding sideways, threatening to whirl itself around as she spun the steering wheel in a sense of slow motion, finally lifting her panicked foot from where it had met the brake. Helmut swung back around and plowed into the bank by the roadside, slamming to a jolting halt. The car's tires whirred uselessly before it stalled.

After several attempts to dislodge the car, she climbed out and leaned heavily against the door, fright still coursing through her quaking limbs.

Tess hugged the side of the road as she started out, walking with careful steps, face stung by the snow. She began to despair of reaching her goal as she pushed on through the blackness.

The mailbox was barely visible, the drive a narrow strip of white through the dark trees when she clambered over the mountain of snow at the foot of it. Her fingers were brittle with cold inside her sodden gloves. Her ears throbbed from the bite of the wind.

At last, she saw specks of light, smeary in the squalls of snow.

Any remnant of fear, uncertainty, had been eclipsed by her desperate need for warmth and shelter. She raised her fist to pound on the door. The handle was unyielding under her hand as she knocked again and again.

Chapter 14

Evan detected a series of distant, repeating sounds as he bent over the sander in his workshop. He switched it off as he yanked his headphones down around his neck.

He listened, and when the sounds came again, he set the sander down and limped out toward the front door.

His duffle was still on the living-room floor, clothes dangling out crazily. He hadn't bothered to unpack, just grabbed whatever he needed as he needed it.

He hadn't decided whether he would stay or go back up north. His life felt just as indecisive, like he was trying to live in two different places simultaneously.

He had left his shirt off in the heat of the stove and his labor and an icy blast struck him when he hauled the door open. Tess's face startled him as he took in her huddled form.

"Come in." He guided her across the threshold. "Not much of a night to be out," he said as he shut the door on the wind's fury.

He reached to take her things and recoiled when icy drops flicked against him. "You're soaked!"

He took her coat and scarf, holding them away from him as he carried them to a chair near the stove, where he spread them to dry.

"How long were you out there?"

"I don't know. A while. My car got stuck."

"What? Where is it?"

"Too far to do anything about right now." She raised her eyes to his. "Evan, I just couldn't wait, not one more day. I had to find a way to see you. Talk with you."

"I'm sorry you were out there in the cold," he said. "I didn't know

I'd locked the door. I was working ..."

"I know I shouldn't just show up like this, but I didn't know what else to do."

Her voice broke then, and she sniffed back a looming sob.

He stepped forward toward her quickly and guided her wordlessly to the couch, then stood back and pressed a hand against his chest as he glanced about the room. Remembering the headphones around his neck, he reached to pull them off and tossed them onto a chair nearby.

"Give me a minute to get some clothes on. I'll be right back." He bolted toward the bedroom.

•

Tess's heart was pounding as she huddled on the couch, her mind reacquainting itself with the sound of his voice, the intensity of his eyes. She was having difficulty meeting them.

"Storm getting bad?" he asked as he loped back into the room a short time later.

She nodded, wishing she didn't feel quite so much like she was meeting him for the first time, clenching her teeth to stop them from chattering.

He pulled a chair near the woodstove and patted the seat. "Here, come sit where it's warm."

She stood and moved to the chair. Her gaze traveled around the room and fixed on the duffle with its overflowing contents, which Evan had now dragged to one side of the room.

He moved toward the kitchen, tucking his shirttails in as he went. He returned with a mug from which the tag of a teabag trailed like a flag. His face looked tired as he filled the cup with water from a kettle steaming on the woodstove then handed it to her.

She thanked him and took several noisy swallows.

He disappeared into his workroom and returned with a cup of his own.

"So." He retrieved the headphones as he lowered himself onto the chair across from her. "How's business?"

"Just the same."

He nodded as his gaze took her in frankly. He sipped a mouthful of tea and held it thoughtfully before setting the cup down on a small table beside him. "You must really have something on your mind to come all the way out here." He gestured toward the window. "In this."

She swallowed hard. "I wasn't sure when I'd see you."

He shrugged without looking at her. "I guess I wasn't, either."

Hurt flashed inside her as she dropped her gaze. "I need very much to talk with you."

His hands pressed the disks of the headphones' earpieces together and apart between his widespread knees as his mouth tightened in a weary sigh.

"Evan, three people who care about you are feeling absolutely rotten. You're the only one who can help us out."

She lifted her heavy damp hair from where it was coiled against her neck and let it fall down her back. "You can blame the whole thing on me, if you like, but please don't break Rowan's heart. I think if he'd understood what this would do to you, he'd never have let it happen. Please, make peace with him."

Evan tipped his head back and studied her.

"Believe me, I had no idea how hard this thing with Celia's paintings would be for you."

He averted his eyes quickly at the sound of the name. "Well, now you do."

"Not really. Not fully."

"No?" His brows raised slowly.

"No, quite truthfully, I don't. I think those paintings are some of the most beautiful I've ever seen. And in a way, you're a part of them. That's what matters to me." She shook her head in exasperation. "I wish I did understand."

"Look." Impatience tinged his voice. "Maybe I'm a little pissed off to find you tangled up in this part of my life when I've tried not to drag you into it, all right?"

"Where else should I be?" she asked indignantly.

He didn't answer or look at her. Instead, his eyes followed the slow arc the headphones made as he twirled them absently.

"Perhaps you simply want me out of your life," she said finally.

He shrugged. "If that's what you want."

"Evan, how can you even imagine that? Do I have to beg you to help me understand?"

His gaze wandered to the window, where windblown snow was an impenetrable curtain of white. "Tess ... do you think I haven't thought about this? Agonized over it?"

"Then why not talk with me about it?"

He shook his head slowly.

"All you have to do is tell me," she urged.

The aqua eyes flashed up as he tossed the headphones aside. "You think it's that easy?"

"It's easier to just shut me out instead?"

The planes of his pallid face seemed especially prominent. "Easier than watching you back away from me like I'm a criminal," he said finally, his voice low.

"I'm convinced that your only crimes are against yourself." She drew her chin upward as her eyes challenged him. "And I'm not going anywhere until I get what I came here for. You'll have to throw me out bodily."

Humor softened his features briefly as he met her eyes. "I don't know if I've got the strength for that."

"Whatever it is, I'm asking for it, Evan." She studied the small tight lines around his eyes as he raked fingers through his tawny hair. "How long are you going to try and keep the beach ball down?"

He glanced up, his expression uncomprehending.

"It always pops up someplace else. Isn't that what you told me?"

He winced as he massaged his left knee vigorously, avoiding her eyes.

She could feel him drawing away from her, from everything, and she longed to impart some sense of safety. "I don't think you've been very fair to yourself, though I don't understand why." Her heart ached as she willed him to look at her. "Please, Evan. I love you so much. Let it go. Be free of it."

He squeezed his eyes shut and pressed a fist against his lips. His breaths were audible now, like someone staving off pain.

Her urge to move closer was overruled by the powerful invisible wall she could feel around him. Her fingers twined together anxiously in her lap as she waited for the move only he could make.

He raised his head, at last. "You know," his gaze stared past her in memory as he drew a deep breath and released it in a long, forceful sigh. "There was one physical therapist who used to really work me hard. When I finally got so exhausted I couldn't see straight, she'd try to get me to talk about how I got hurt."

Amazement touched his features as he recalled, "She had the

courage to ask me about it outright, while the rest of them tiptoed around me like some kind of time bomb."

His mouth twisted in a sad smile. "She said I should try to make the pieces fit. I told her then that there were too many of them missing."

He rubbed his leg furiously as he struggled with his thoughts.

"What I had with Celia began so early. It seems like it was always there, as far back as I can remember."

His lips pursed in memory. "At seventeen she was … as beautiful as those paintings that seemed to just flow from something deep inside her. A place I could never reach. I figured it was only a matter of time before we'd finally be on our own and be able to join our lives together.

"But her family decided differently. Found all kinds of ways to keep us apart. I guess you could say they didn't take much to my background." A small knot of muscle twitched in his jaw. "They didn't pay her much attention, but they always made sure she never had any choices.

"I thought things would finally all work out when we were both at school in Boston. But then I began to realize that there was this unhappiness in her, and nothing could seem to make better. She had a dependence on me—on our relationship—that I knew was bad, but I let it go on."

Tess startled a little when he glanced up at her suddenly. The look in his eyes spawned a lump in her throat.

"For a long time, I was convinced that if I just made her feel loved enough, we could get past it somehow. Her work, her career, became the focal point of everything for us, but other than that, there wasn't much left. I watched her get more and more restless, more detached from reality, and saw that really it seemed worst when she was with me. She seemed more—connected—when she was with others, especially the new friends she was making. I decided to get out of the picture, give her space to build her life. She said she wanted that.

"I went south, but she soon came down to find me. The old restlessness came back before long, and I decided again that we'd be better apart. That's when I went to Europe."

He opened his mouth to continue, then closed his eyes with a protracted sigh. "I told myself that I was doing it for her. I wanted to believe that. But I knew by that time that she couldn't really manage on her own. She had lived with me, but we weren't ... lovers anymore. I was still in love with somebody who didn't seem to exist. And I couldn't seem to handle what—who—was there in its place. The responsibility was getting so constant. And the part of me that still wanted a marriage, that still wanted that dream I'd had all those years, kept denying what was happening."

He rose laboriously to his feet. His limp was pronounced as he moved toward the front door and stood with his forehead pressed against the glass.

"I got away, but I wasn't free. I felt more incomplete than ever. Always wanting what she'd been, and worrying about her. She answered my letters maybe every third or fourth time, and there were such swings between elation and despair that it was impossible to tell what was really happening.

"Then, just when I was beginning to feel like I could stay on in Spain, I got a call saying that she was coming back here, and wanted me to come back, too. I told her I would if things could really work for us, and she promised that they would. We agreed that it was time we got married. So, we made plans for that."

He turned and laid his palms flat against the door behind him, staring blankly ahead as he summoned memory. "The weekend of our wedding, there was a dance at the Spinnaker—our rehearsal party."

Evan fell silent.

Tess watched his face closely, but said nothing.

"She walked in with someone else, made a big point of introducing him around, then came over and told me that we'd have to talk later, but it looked like the wedding wasn't going to happen after all. That was it for me." His hand made a cutting motion through the air. "I was stupid. I made a big scene. Then I took off. She came by to see me about two the next morning and we took a drive. We went out near Morrison Beach and sat in the car up on the bluffs for hours, trying to get someplace."

He moved away from the door and began to pace, muscles tensing, fingers curling tightly into his palms. He seemed to choose his words with slow, deliberate care. "She was ... frenzied. Her eyes all ... glazed and strange. I tried to hold her but she wouldn't let me, and she wouldn't be still. She was wild—laughing and crying, and angry at me for going away. I kept trying to remind her how it had really been. Tell her that things could be all right if we stayed together, but she said they'd never be right."

His gaze dropped to the floor. "I didn't know then that she was pregnant. I didn't find that out until ... later. I let her pour out her story about Stephen Kearsage, punch holes in my insides with it, and still I offered to take her back, promised to take care of her."

His voice grew deeper, heavy and unsteady. "That's when she laughed at me, screamed at me that I didn't know how, that I'd never know how. That she didn't need me because she'd finally found the man she knew she'd been waiting for all along."

The aqua eyes narrowed with pain. "I was filled with ... blind rage. I wanted to be sure she'd hurt as much as I did."

He raked a hand through his hair. "Oh, God, I knew better. I saw how manic she was, but even that didn't stop me. I made sure she'd never be happy with Stephen."

His features were rigid in memory. "I didn't even know for sure that it was true, but I threw it at her anyway. I spelled it out in all the unpleasant terms I could think of."

He averted his eyes. "I told her just who Stephen was, who her parents really were ..."

"Evan! No!" Tess leaned forward quickly to correct him, thinking of how hard it must have been for Celia to hear the awful truth twice in such a short time, and from Evan, whom she may have hoped would discount it.

Face pale, he continued, "She bolted, then. And I just sat there. I was hurting too much to realize what she was doing—heading for the edge.

"When I did, I tore after her. But it was too late."

He stopped pacing and gripped the back of a chair convulsively. "Evan, please ..."

He went on as though he didn't hear her. "When she turned around, her face was joyous." His own seemed to puzzle painfully at the memory. "I was a hundredth of a second behind her. I remember lunging for her with all I had."

He sat then, and studied his hands in palpable silence. "That air felt so ... empty in my hands." His voice rose on these last words then broke, as a deep sob escaped him.

Tess didn't know how to interrupt him now.

"Everything felt suspended," he said finally. "Then it felt like the whole world broke in two. I was lying on the sand facing her. I remember trying to move, speak, but nothing happened. Just agony. She hadn't missed the rocks the way I had. For a few ridiculous moments, I thought that because I couldn't recognize her, she must be someone else."

He shook his head slowly. "It's crazy, the things we do to keep from believing something too awful. Then I began to realize that probably no one would find us. If the pain didn't push me over first, the tide would get me when it came. Finally the pain made everything black."

He stopped and pressed his hands against his face, releasing a ragged exhalation, half sigh, half sob. Tears coursed silently from his glistening, unfocused eyes.

Tess's voice was locked in her throat. He wouldn't hear, whatever she said. He was held in the horrified thrall of remembered fear and pain. He had no choice but to go on, she realized. He was telling this as much to himself as to her.

He slumped in the chair, muscles collapsing in defeat, gaze fixed to the floor.

Finally, he reached to wipe the dampness from his face. His hands dropped palm upward on his thighs as he continued hoarsely, "At first, the pain from my injuries took a back seat to what I felt inside. Morphine didn't take that away and it followed me everywhere—awake or in dreams that have never stopped since. I suppose I tried hard to simply will myself out of life, for a time. I kept fighting it, and they kept opening me up, to make me better, telling me how lucky I'd be to keep my leg."

His eyes hardened as he remembered, "I was so angry to be alive!" He pressed his eyes shut with a violent shake of his head.

Tess curled tightly into her chair in the silence, pinning her hands between her knees to control the shivering that shook her.

"I finally gave up when I realized there'd be no getting away," he sighed at last. "I discovered that if I worked myself real hard, the pain got so bad, I couldn't think about anything. I could sleep like a dead man and wake up without thinking of her first thing."

The image of his face was becoming blurred for Tess, now.

"You can't escape time pushing you on, putting other stuff to think about in your way," he said. "It was painful, getting back to things, but I think maybe it also helped keep me alive. I worked at the mill to pay off most of the bills, and finally got enough stashed aside so I could come back here and work on my own."

His thoughtful face bore the trace of a smile. "It's amazing what a refuge day-to-day's can become."

He rose again and went to the door, placing his hands high on either side of its frame as he looked out. The evidence of strength in his back and arms was indistinct through the moisture that was spilling out of Tess's eyes.

"It's been almost five years now. There's not a day I don't think about all the things I didn't do. Though not half as much as I think of what I did do," he finished quietly.

Tess longed to help staunch his pain, but couldn't push words past the constriction in her throat. With a numb sense of helplessness, she watched as he put on the jacket that hung near the door. His eyes were like polished stones as he looked at her.

Before she could speak, he was gone, head bowed as he stepped outside and was swallowed by the squalls of swirling snow.

He didn't want her to stop him or follow him, she knew. He had let go of too much pain here not to feel trapped. The storm was his only escape, and she had to allow him that.

Had to allow, as she wept freely now, that it was his to get through the worst of his own storm, and hers to wait till it had passed.

Chapter 15

Evan's heart threatened to burst inside him as he tore across the field toward the shore. Snow stung the eyes already blinded by tears as he trudged through the endless white, knee-deep in spots, his leg protesting angrily as it slid out from under him.

He walked for a long time, following an internal guide that drew him to the very spot to which he had never been able to return. One by one, his thoughts lighted on different faces, settings, and all the things that he had wanted—all the things that had never been. Would never be.

The sand and water were obscured from his view as he stood on the bluff above the cove that formed Morrison Beach. The wind whipped the snow around fiercely, buffeting him as he stood rigid, like a sentry, waiting.

It took a long time. When it came, it was long and hard and aching, far away, at first. It rose and fell, carried away and back again above the wind's roar like the tide. His inner ear drew it in, finally, following it, puzzling over it, till at last he knew the source.

It was as though he watched from some point above it all, watched the figure battered by snow, down on its knees, face contorted in a release of agony, the sound of pain pouring out as though it would never stop.

His own voice. That of a frightened child, grief-stricken adolescent, and at long last, fully shattered man. Crying out from the hole that had splintered open in his chest, from what welled out of him as he gasped into sobs that pulled him together whole once again, shook him back into awareness that it was all happening to him, right here. That, in this moment, he was that pain.

There was nothing left but to be this. The world went away, and this was all there was. He had been, surely would be, this forever.

•

Tess sat still in the chair for what seemed like hours, remembering his words, his face. Feeling his pain wash through her.

Scenes of the day at Morrison Beach reeled through her imagination, interspersed with her new understanding of Evan's supreme sacrifice, of the long years of tortured guilt he'd spent here.

She was filled with shame at her doubts about this man who'd been so incapable of inflicting possible hurt in absolving himself that he'd lived in lonely pain, instead.

Her face was swollen and her head throbbed by the time she finally became conscious of the wind's loud moaning. She startled each time it rattled the front door, disappointed when it didn't yield Evan after all.

Where could he have gone? What if something had happened, if the storm was even worse than she could perceive from here? What if he was in trouble somewhere?

A cold dread overtook her when an ugly suggestion insinuated itself. What if he didn't come back? What if it had all been more than he could bear, what if—she shook the thought away.

No sense thinking this way, yet she couldn't seem to stop.

In an instant, the lights went out and her heart leapt inside her. She groped blindly in the darkness, her head spinning with accumulated exhaustion. She misjudged her bearings and felt a door handle beneath her hand. She turned it slowly and edged inside.

The room was very cold. Her knees bumped the edge of the bed and she reached out, feeling the cool smoothness of the coverlet under her hands.

She pulled it back and slid beneath, drawing its heavy bulk over her and dropping her head to a down pillow that held the same clean smell as Evan's clothes.

It seemed right that she should curl here, be where he would seem closest when he felt so far away.

Had she ever loved anyone the way her heart felt about him now, like it had brimmed full?

In the kind of inner decision that was often her sincerest prayer, she told herself, "I have to trust he'll get through this. That he's protected. He'll come back. All I can do is wait here, with all this love I feel. What I thought I could never, ever feel again."

Suddenly, she remembered something Andy had woken one day and told her shortly before he died: *You have to believe what your heart loves, what it wants. As hard as you can, with everything you've got. That's the way love comes into the world.*

Slowly, her thoughts quieted to a distant buzz, then a stillness, as sleep overtook her tired limbs. She dozed in fitful snatches, bolting awake at the sounds of the wind as it rattled about the house.

Over and over again, she woke to tell him that everything was all right, to share the truth that would clarify what he had misunderstood.

Dreams mimicked her waking thoughts as they had her telling him again and again until, at last, deep exhaustion triumphed and she slept dreamlessly.

•

Almost an hour had passed when Evan realized that both of his knees were locked with stiffness. His mouth tasted of salt and steel cold, and his head was as numb as his limbs, dulled with a sleepy stillness he immediately recognized as dangerous.

His arms were next to useless as he struggled to his feet, which promptly slid out from underneath him. He paused, drawing deep breaths, summoning what strength remained.

His left leg screamed in outrage as he yanked himself upward, battling the spinning in his brain. His legs still felt as lifeless as dolls, and it was only with measured, meager steps that he was able to move forward, knowing that he might not get up if he lost his footing again.

Everything left in him was concentrated on staggering ahead with dogged steps until the circulation seeped painfully back into his limbs as he worked them through the depth of the snow.

When he pressed his chin deeper into his collar, he found that frost had already formed on his face.

Nothing had ever seemed so important as being on the other side of this pain for good, and now, less than a half mile from home, he realized he might not make it. Cold and exhaustion were dimming his thoughts, and he was starting to stumble.

He pulled himself up sharply and thought instantly of a time many years before when he and his father had gotten caught out in a storm. The older man had hoisted the small boy to his shoulders when he'd grown too cold and tired to take another step.

From the seat aloft his father's weary back, Evan had counted the steps aloud in a series of tens until they'd arrived home a long time later.

"Keep going, keep going!" his father had cried out over the howling wind each time Evan had stopped.

It was his father's voice he heard in his ears now as he counted each successive painful step, knowing that more than anything he wanted to get back or die trying.

At last, the house appeared as a dark mass through the snow that whirled across the fields. The Volvo stood alone, blanketed in white.

Disappointment stung his heart. Always alone. There was an ache in his throat, but nothing left to push it away.

He sighed in resignation, his thoughts as weary and heavy as his legs. His heart.

He collapsed inside the door, fingers clawing for the switch beside it, surprised to find that it yielded no light.

Then his thoughts registered the problem, the result of the storm's fury, and he groped toward the counter near the sink, his hand closing around a small kerosene lamp. His whole frame shook as his fingers fumbled with the wooden matches he found beside it. Finally he got its wick lit.

The light seemed brilliant to his eyes, so accustomed to the darkness. The flame cast huge shadows on the wall as he stripped off his stiff, sodden clothes near the woodstove.

He carried the lamp to the bathroom where he put on a pair of sweat pants and pulled on a heavy sweater.

In the living room, he found his cup and moved toward the woodstove, filling it with water from the kettle. He clasped the cup tightly with both hands as he took long swallows, steam stinging the frostiness on his face.

Disbelief drew the furrow between his brows when his gaze lighted on Tess's coat, scarf, and gloves where he'd spread them on a chair beside the stove earlier. The wool was warm and dry beneath his hand when he touched it.

He pictured her hurrying out into the storm after him and fear flooded him before he realized that she must still be here.

He reached for the lamp eagerly and moved toward the back of the house. The flickering light cast a smaller glow before him as he approached the bedroom. When he raised the lantern high to hook its handle on a nail in the beam overhead, his tired eyes found her at last.

Her dark hair half-veiled her face, so pale in sleep. So childlike.

In the dim light, Celia's painting glowed over the bed where Tess lay curled under the covers.

Celia's wonderful work, he marveled. Almost as wonderful as this woman who seemed to love it—and him—so much.

He shook his head in amazement.

She was here. She had stayed. Had waited for him, after all.

He felt a warm expansion near his heart as he studied her face in an overwhelming rush of love, unwilling to disturb her, wanting this moment to last forever.

He forgot all about the icy cold that had gripped him as he lowered himself down beside the bed until his face was level with hers.

She stirred softly, full mouth moving, forming silent words.

He reached and pushed locks of hair back from her face with trembling fingers.

Her lids shot open. "Claire ..." Her voice was heavy with sleep as she worked to get the word out.

"It's all right," he soothed, smoothing her hair across the pillow. "We'll call her when the power's back. Go back to sleep."

Her hand flew out and clutched at his sleeve, eyes wide and determined.

He froze in surprise, had to crane his head to make out her words at first, as she whispered them.

"She knew." Tess's unfocused eyes seemed panicked as she forced them open. "Already knew—Celia."

Her head dropped back with the effort, and she struggled to raise it.

He watched her, confused.

" ... must listen." Her hoarse voice was insistent as it rose slowly from a whisper, rushed on, as though frantic to get the words out. "Claire'd already told her—told Celia. Knew she ... had to be told."

Tess struggled into a sitting position, her hair a tumbled mass around her small face as her hands gripped his arms desperately, hanging onto him as though he would float away.

"You have to understand. Celia already knew. Claire had already told her ..."

Stunned by her words, he watched her silently

"If you'd only known all this time. Please, you've got to believe me." Her eyes were filled with tears. "Please ... don't go away. I couldn't bear ..." Her voice gave way as the tears came quickly.

"No. Oh, no," he cried. "Tess. I'm not going anywhere. I'm right here."

Warm moisture stung his eyes again and trickled down his face as he silenced her mouth with his own, astonished at her words, that she had spoken them to him. Their limbs became a tangle as he clung to her feverishly, then pulled her against him until their hearts were pressed together.

"There. Just like this," he gasped against her hair. "I could never leave you."

He rocked her back and forth as her limbs warmed him.

"I can't believe that you're here," he said at last.

"Of course I'm here," she said, impatience darting through her slurred voice. "I'm always going to be here, unless you send me away."

He kissed her lingeringly then, holding her face in his hands breathlessly as though he'd never have enough of her.

"Do you understand what I said?" She pulled away, drawing herself up onto her elbow, staring into his eyes.

"It's almost too much to understand. But I heard you, yes."

"It's different now," she told him insistently.

"Yes, it's quite different." He smiled quickly. "Now I'm the one who's afraid I'm going to wake up soon."

"You're so cold." Her hands smoothed his face.

He caught one of them and kissed it, then released it and rose slowly, moving toward the lamp.

He lifted it down and set it on the floor beside the bed. "Where on earth is your car?"

"Keeping the snow fences company. I was determined to get here. I got good and stuck."

She lay back against the pillows with a tiny smile that tugged at his heart.

"Nothing would have dared get in your way." He shook his head with a smile. "I don't see any way we can get you home tonight."

She reached across the bed and extinguished the lamp with a quick breath. Then from the darkness, she asked softly whether she wasn't there already.

He found her then, and knew that it was true.

•••

Phyllis Edgerly Ring

Phyllis Edgerly Ring left part of her heart in her childhood home of Germany, which she visits as often as she can. She loves writing, travel, and the noblest possibilities in the human heart. She is always curious to discover how history, culture, relationship, spirituality, and the natural world influence us and point the way for the human family on its shared journey.

She has worked as writer, editor, nurse, tour guide, program director at a Baha'i conference center, taught English to kindergartners in China, and served as instructor for the Long Ridge Writer's Group. She has written for such publications as Christian Science Monitor, Ms., Writer's Digest, and Yankee, worked as editor for several publications, and published two nonfiction books about creating balance between the spiritual and material requirements of life. She and her husband live in New Hampshire, happy to be near their grown children —some of the most thoughtful people they know.

CPSIA information can be obtained at www.ICGtesting.com
Printed in the USA
LVOW06s0240050114

368082LV00001B/27/P